THE LORD

THE TENTH DAY

DANICA FAVORITE

Cover design by EDHGraphics
Edited by Laurie Kuna

This book is a work of fiction. Names, characters, places, and incidents either are products of the author's imagination or are used fictitiously. Any resemblance to actual persons, living or dead, events, or locales is entirely coincidental.

ISBN Print: 978-1-945079-03-0

Visit my website at www.danicafavorite.com

Printed in the United States of America

Twelve men. Twelve brides. Twelve days to save a town.

Christmas, 1876: Noelle, Colorado is in danger of becoming a ghost town if the railroad decides to bypass the mountaintop mining community. Determined to prove their town is thriving, twelve men commit to ordering brides before the railroad's deadline six days into the New Year.

Each of the twelve women has her own reason for signing up to become a mail-order bride. But after they arrive in the uncivilized settlement, they aren't so sure they've made the right decision. Neither are the grooms.

Will the marriages happen in time to save Noelle?

About the book:

On the tenth day of Christmas, my true love gave to me...

Desperately trying to avoid an arranged marriage to a cruel lord, an heiress takes on Minnie Gold's identity to marry a man she hopes will be kind. He has to be better than what her parents have planned.

Hugh Montgomery is proud of the life he's built in Noelle, and he's determined to help Noelle survive- even if it means taking on a mail-order bride. Burned by love, he knows marriage is about commitment and companionship and is looking forward to sharing his life with someone who doesn't expect his heart.

However, when a woman from Hugh's past arrives, she reveals secrets that Hugh and Minnie were desperate to hide. Hugh can't marry Minnie, knowing her true identity, but he also can't let her return home. As Hugh and Minnie fight to save their respective futures, will the growing affection between them ruin everything? Or can they find a way to build a future together?

CHAPTER 1

NOELLE, COLORADO

DECEMBER 24TH, 1876

Minnie Gold was a fraud. Those were the whispers, and as much as Minnie tried to ignore them, she couldn't deny they were the truth. The trouble with living a lie was that having gotten to know the other mail-order brides in her group, Minnie was developing a fondness for the other women. They were all here to make a better life for themselves, something which Minnie could relate to.

But after watching Maybelle throw a fit because this trip wasn't living up to the lifestyle she wanted, Minnie was afraid to tell the truth. Would these women respect her if they found out that the only reason she'd fallen into the scheme was to avoid a fate not of her own choosing? What would they say when they knew what had happened to the real Minnie Gold?

It wasn't as though she'd killed Minnie. On the contrary.

Margaret Coveney had done everything she could to save her maid. No, not her maid. Her friend. It was true that Minnie had been employed by Margaret's family to take care of Margaret and her needs. But being of similar age and interest, Margaret and Minnie had become far more than that. And now Minnie was dead, and Margaret was pretending to be her.

Minnie sighed as she looked down at the tattered gloves she wore. She hadn't had a choice, and the real Minnie had begged her to do this.

It had been a mistake coming here. But what other choice did she have? Minnie rubbed her arms. She hadn't expected it to be so cold, which was foolish, if she had stopped to think about it. After all, they were in the mountains, beyond the snowcapped peaks she could see in the distance from her former home in Denver. Of course, she would have been cold in the snow. But the real Minnie hadn't had anything warm in her belongings. It shamed her to think of how poorly she had treated her faithful servant. Not that she had ever mistreated Minnie. She had always given the other girl her cast-offs, thinking she was doing her a kindness. And she supposed she was, but of what use were ball gowns, afternoon dresses, and all the other fancy things she'd had in her wardrobe? If she could go back and do it all over, she would have thought about practical things to give her maid. She pulled the shawl tighter around her. If only she had ruined one of her fur-lined capes.

One of the women, Birdie, handed her a roll of cloth. "Here. Take this. It will warm you."

Minnie smiled at her. "You are too kind."

Birdie shook her head. "There's no such thing as being too kind. Besides, I don't want you catching your death. It would be a shame to have gone to all this trouble for nothing."

So true. It would be a shame to have gone to all this

trouble only to freeze to death. Still, as the wagon pulled into the tiny town of Noelle, Colorado, Minnie couldn't help wondering if she had chosen wrong.

Of what use was a husband she didn't know, in comparison to one she would? They said gambling was a sin, but wasn't this just a gamble as well? The pompous Lord Milliken her mother wanted her to marry might be rich, but he was an evil person. Minnie shook her head. No, he wasn't even rich. He just had the title and was gladly trading it for her parents' fortune. A complete wastrel, by every definition, and according to the real Minnie, a man who could not be trusted around women.

Margaret gazed at the eager looking faces of the men who had gathered. Which one in the group was she to marry? The one who she and Minnie had chosen for the maid? Margaret knew, of course, all about Minnie's plan to join a group of mail-order brides to start a new life for herself. After all, it had been Margaret who encouraged her. Minnie had confessed a deep fear of Margaret's intended and told she not to marry him. Margaret's parents weren't giving her a choice. Once the holidays were over, Margaret was supposed to be traveling to England with Lord Millikin to be married. Even though Lord Millikin had told her she'd be allowed to bring her maid, there was something about the fear in Minnie's eyes that made Margaret hesitate.

She'd always suspected that there was more to Minnie's fear than she'd let on, but she'd never pressed her. Instead, she'd helped Minnie secure a place among the Lost Lambs where she could have a husband who would be kind to her and provide her with a good life. Minnie had often told Margaret that such a thing was far better than anything she could've hoped for herself, to have a good husband to care for her. Both women had agreed that by going through a benevolent society such as this, it was assured that the men would be good, kind, faithful Christians.

She'd just never expected that in helping Minnie choose a husband, she was actually choosing her own. But as she looked at the faces, she had a hard time picturing any of them as kind, decent, Christian men. Most looked like they hadn't had a bath in a long time. Such were the sort that she avoided encountering on the street in Denver. Her parents had always cautioned her against such men, and this was one area in which both Margaret and Minnie agreed with them.

When she did have the misfortune of encountering them, they would call out to her, saying vulgar things. Some were often so bold as to try to touch her. To feel the soft silk of her dress, or, even worse, her beautiful golden hair. That's what everyone wanted to know. Were those silky tresses made of gold?

She shook her head. Such simpletons. Minnie, too, had the same color hair. And often, people mistook them for sisters instead of maid and mistress. Secretly, she had always wished for Minnie to be her sister. A sister would have been so lovely, to have someone to confide secrets to like sisters do. Minnie had been that to her, but sometimes, she felt that Minnie didn't fully understand her. When she would complain of the many balls she'd been forced to attend, Minnie had sighed longingly, and she had always felt guilty. But for a difference in their status of birth, Margaret got to go to the balls, when she wished she could have stayed home, and Minnie was forced to remain behind while longing to go.

At least there would be no balls in Noelle. No, not a one. There wasn't even a sufficient looking building to host such an event. It would be nice to have some vestige of civilization, however. Once the snow melted, this place would be covered in mud, and there weren't even sidewalks to protect her skirts.

"Minnie. Minnie!"

It took her a moment to realize that they were referring to her. Yes. Right. She was Minnie now. How easily she'd forgotten. How could she view this place through Minnie's eyes? To Margaret, it was a step down. But to Minnie, perhaps it was a step up.

She took a deep breath. She was not Margaret anymore. Minnie. Yes. Yes, she was Minnie.

She gave the gentleman a smile. "Yes. I'm Minnie Gold. Are you my intended?"

The man looked at her as though he wasn't sure what to expect. What to make of her. Did she displease him in some way? So soon?

"Indeed I am. I'm Hugh Montgomery. I must say, you aren't what I was expecting."

Trying to remember to be Minnie, she took a deep breath. "And what were you expecting? I believe I have given you a great deal of information about myself. There wasn't time for proper courtship."

Hugh shook his head. "You seem rather highborn."

Highborn? Considering this man spoke like the English lord she'd been running from, she could make the same statement about him. Yet no one would expect someone of rank to be living in such a dismal place. Which was why it was a place perfect for her to hide.

But he did have a point. Because she'd slipped into speaking as Margaret, not Minnie. Although, Minnie wasn't so low as one would assume. After all, she had been educated right alongside Margaret, had tended to every one of her whims, and accompanied her to a good many events. Minnie wasn't her equal, at least in terms of how society viewed her, but she had been given many of the same advantages as Margaret.

"I wasn't aware that education and breeding were something to find fault with. I was raised alongside my mistress, as her mother felt it would be good for me to be educated in a like manner so that I wouldn't pass on any undesirable qualities to her child."

At least that was the truth. How many times had her mother gone on and on and on about wanting her to remain perfectly unspoiled? She'd frowned upon her closeness with her maid, and the girls often hid their friendship from others. It had been such a burden on her, and as she calmly repeated her mother's words, she felt guilty about how it must have injured Minnie. Dear, sweet Minnie.

Hugh frowned. "I see. From where did they get you?"

That she wasn't sure. Nor did she think Minnie would know because Minnie had come to them at such a young age.

"I was brought to their home as a small child. I believe the goal was to give their daughter someone to keep her company, as there were to be no more children."

Another statement from her mother that had always made her feel bad. Her family had put so much pressure on her as their only child. One more reason to feel guilty. They were counting on her to marry well, but she couldn't marry a man who made her skin crawl, and her parents thought she was being overdramatic.

"So, you know nothing of your family? Your people?"

Talk about being highbrow. Who did this man think she he was, questioning her origins? He was worse than her parents, grilling potential suitors over their acceptability for marrying into the Coveney fortune. Only this man had no fortune. No title.

"It is not something that has ever been spoken of in my presence. And I can't imagine why it would matter so much to you." She frowned at him. "After all, you mentioned nothing in your letter about requiring a specific pedigree."

A smile crossed Hugh's lips. "Indeed. I have no use for someone with a pedigree, as you say. I was merely curious because it seems odd, that is all."

"I'm sorry for displeasing you," she said.

Hugh shook his head. "No, you do not. I suppose I had formed a different expectation."

That didn't sound good either. But how well could you know a person from a letter? Still, she wished they had thought to have asked for a photograph or something. Perhaps then they would have been able to discern the disapproving look on the man's face. Minnie hadn't been expecting someone who was overly handsome, though looks didn't entirely matter. Except when one wore an expression of such disapproval that Margaret feared she had been sending her maid into a place worse than the one they had left.

"Allow me to escort you inside," Hugh said, offering an arm gallantly. And yet, the welcoming gesture did not reach his face.

Margaret took his arm and went inside with him.

"I don't approve of this, not at all," Hugh said. "Though I know that not all the women here, including yourself, are expecting a fine mansion, I do apologize for the accommodations. Temporary as though they may be, they are not entirely suited to a woman about to embark upon a married life."

Ugh. The same propriety she had heard from many of the prospective grooms her parents had tried setting her up with. Apparently, she couldn't run from propriety. What was wrong with plain speech and leaving behind the formalities of the world?

Minnie could read French well enough to understand the

7

name of the place they were staying. *La Maison des Chats*. Such a place would have horrified her mother, and frankly, if her reputation were not already ruined by going on this adventure, setting foot in such a place would finish the job. There was no going back now. As harsh as this man seemed to be, Minnie was stuck marrying him. Margaret could be no more.

A naked man ran past her, and Hugh quickly stepped between them to shield her. No, she could not return to her old life.

Minnie gingerly stepped into the parlor. "I'm sure it will suit just fine," she said. "After all, it is only temporary, is it not? I'm assuming you have alternative accommodations for after our wedding."

Hugh gave a slow nod. "It's not much, just a set of rooms off my office. But it's close enough, and will keep you warm for the winter."

That was all Minnie had wanted. A safe place to live, and someone to care for her. It was clear Hugh was just as disappointed in Minnie as she was in him, but surely, he could at least be kind.

Please Lord, let him be kind.

The gypsy woman, Kezia, struggled with a bundle as her baby in her other arm fussed.

"May I take her for you?" Minnie asked, holding out her arms.

Kezia gave her an odd look. "Do you know anything about babies?"

She could feel Hugh's eyes on her. He was expecting a maid, a woman who could help him through the trials of life. She'd never held a baby, too many germs according to her mother. But she loved babies and had always been curious about them.

"I should like to learn," she said. "As a maid to a young

lady, I didn't have much opportunity. But they are darling, and your little Jem seems like an angel."

The other woman made a noise and handed the baby to her. She held the baby as she'd seen Kezia do. Something in her heart gave a funny twist as the child smiled up at her. She hadn't wanted children for herself, not with all her mother's warnings about the diseases and the inconveniences. In particular, she'd been dreading the wedding night, an act necessary for the begetting of children. Her mother had told her that it was a most demeaning and humiliating experience, and that she should drink plenty of wine beforehand, but not so much that she got sick, and it would make the act more bearable. Minnie had told her that some of the maids would giggle about how wonderful it was, and that it couldn't be so terrible if women led lives of sin. Sometimes, the girls would look through the books in her father's study to find a definitive answer.

But as her wedding day drew closer, Minnie hadn't been as interested in finding out the truth. Instead, she'd told Margaret not to waste time on such nonsense, and that if she was set on going through with her parents' plans, she should take her mother's advice. And perhaps, spend a great deal of time in prayer.

Cuddling Jem close to her, she inhaled her sweet scent. Perhaps a few moments of humiliation would be worth it to have such bliss.

"You're looking forward to children, then?" Hugh asked.

Margaret stared at him. With such a cold expression, would Hugh be any different in the marital bed?

Already, there was talk of postponing the weddings to give the brides the chance to get to know the grooms. How long could Margaret, er Minnie, put off the inevitable?

"In due time," she said.

One of the colorful women whose rooms they'd taken

over passed by. Her dress was scandalous, her manner even more so as she looked at Hugh.

"Do you know her?" Minnie asked.

The baby gave a small squawk as if she also wished to know the answer. Hugh turned red.

"We're... acquainted..." He said.

Minnie frowned. "So long as you choose not to continue that acquaintance upon our marriage."

Margaret's mother had told her that it was best to turn a blind eye to a husband's indiscretions. That advice had come after Margaret had seen Lord Milliken leave a place similar to this, a scantily clad woman waving to him out the window.

Both Margaret and Minnie had agreed that if a man could not honor his marriage vows, he was not an honorable man at all. One more reason the idea of marrying Lord Milliken had seemed insufferable.

But once again, Margaret had to wonder if marrying a man whose character she knew so little about would only be inviting more of the same that she had left.

HUGH CLOSED his eyes and squeezed the bridge of his nose as he thought about how to handle the situation. While it was true that he had visited some of Madame's girls in the past, he'd found the experience lacking. And Angelique, who had just passed, was less of a lover and more of a friend. He paid for her time because it was the gentlemanly thing to do, but mostly, talking to Angelique was better than talking to a priest. He could tell her anything, and rather than being bound by a vague promise to a God that Hugh had no trust in, Angelique would keep his secrets because she couldn't speak. Besides, Angelique was barely older than a child, and

Hugh could not see himself pressing a man's needs upon one.

"I can assure you that I believe in being faithful to one's marriage vows," he said. "However, Angelique is a dear friend, and while I understand that in a larger town, status and social class being what they are, such an acquaintance is frowned upon. Here in Noelle, there are few opportunities for friendship. I would think, given that in your previous life, your status created a similar division in opportunities for friendship, you would be more inclined to giving Angelique a chance."

The other women in the room gasped, and Hugh fought the urge to groan. He'd left England precisely to rid himself of the chains of class division. A man's worth came from his accomplishments in life, not the manor he was or was not born to. At least that was how things worked in Noelle, which was why Hugh had been willing to stay and help this town fulfill Charlie Hardt's vision.

He'd hoped, by marrying a maid, he could once and for all be done with the judgments that came with one's position in society.

Unfortunately, he'd somehow ended up with a maid whose snobbishness nearly matched that of his highly-esteemed, titled, family he'd deliberately left behind in England in search of a new life. Not that any of them cared that he'd gone to the wilds of America. As the third son of a Duke, the family was delighted to have him out of the way. Every good nobleman needs an heir and a spare, but when one was as fertile as his parents, the additional sons were more of a burden.

At least Minnie appeared to be embarrassed. "You are right, of course. It will take time to get used to this new way of living. I hope I did not cause too much offense."

"Why should you be worried about what some low-class

woman of the night thinks of you? True, you're just a maid. At least you're able to better your position by marrying up." One of the woman, Maybelle, he believed, turned and gave Hugh a disgusted look before looking at Minnie again. "Fortunately for you, moving up doesn't take much."

Hopefully, the women hadn't become friends on the journey. He wasn't sure he could enjoy having such a woman in his home as a guest.

The baby fussed in Minnie's arms, and she worked to console her. For someone who didn't have experience with babies, He had to admit that she was a natural. Perhaps in time, they could work out their personality differences enough to create a happy family of their own.

Kezia returned to the room and took the baby. "It is past time she eats. Thank you for your help."

Minnie gave her a smile that stirred something inside Hugh. Like there were qualities deep within her worth getting to know.

"Of course. I'm willing to help anytime. As my future husband says, we are in a new place, with limited resources. We should do what we can to help one another as we are able."

Perhaps he had been too hasty to judge her. He'd mostly been excited to draw the straw for her because on paper, she seemed very qualified to do the job. A maid would be familiar with a rougher lifestyle, knowing how to cook, clean, and take care of things around their home. But he hadn't thought about what kind of person she might be. Silly, considering the whole reason he had embarked on his adventure was to focus more on a person's character than on a person's status. He was just as guilty of the snobbery which he seemed so intent on turning his back upon. He'd seen the word, maid, in the description of the bride, and assumed she'd be exactly what he wanted.

The other women murmured like they agreed with her statement. Minnie looked around, then sat upon one of the velvet sofas, like she was expecting to be waited upon. An odd gesture for a servant.

"I could so use a cup of tea," she said. "I don't suppose there's anyone here to get it for us."

With a sigh, she stood. "If someone could direct me to the kitchen, I'll see about getting us some refreshment."

He liked that she had included everyone in the offer of tea. And, that once she rightly assumed that there was no one to wait on them, that she was willing to do it. That had to be a good sign, because this was what her life was going to be like. If Noelle returned to its boom status, then there might be additional money to get her some help around the house. But as the assayer, he knew that was unlikely.

As much as Hugh hated to dash Charlie's dreams, the rock from the mine that had been brought to him for inspection was diminishing in value. He'd heard from other assayers across Colorado that the gold in their mines was also petering out. The riches of the mountains would not be found in gold, at least not as far as Hugh could tell. Still, he patiently examined every specimen brought to him, hoping that if not gold, there would be something valuable left in these hills.

Otherwise, Noelle would have to find a new source of wealth. And Hugh feared that even the railroad would not be enough to save them.

But as he looked across the room at all the excited faces, he could not give voice to that fear. It was Christmas Eve. On a night such as this, these good people deserved hope. And until the railroad came, Hugh would keep his fears to himself, standing by his friends and praying he was wrong about his suspicion that all the gold was gone.

When he'd been matched with his bride, he'd thought that

her name, Minnie Gold, was a sign that good fortune was heading their way. But so far, Minnie wasn't what he had expected, and Hugh had to wonder if his hopes of being wrong about the gold were also founded on unrealistic expectations.

CHAPTER 2

THE FIRST DAY OF CHRISTMAS

DECEMBER 25, 1876

The next morning, Hugh invited Minnie to spend some time walking around the town. It would be a good chance for them to get to know one another, and for her to see her new home. Even though she knew she would be alone with him at some point, her stomach was in knots at the prospect.

Now that they were in a warm home instead of bouncing around a wagon, she had hoped to become friends with some of the women. But conversing with them was awkward and stilted. They all seemed to know what she felt inside. Minnie was a fraud. Mostly, they ignored her, except for Maybelle, the horrible snob who seemed to think she was better than everyone else because she came from a good family. Maybelle seemed to think Minnie was her new personal maid.

Ha! If only Minnie dared to tell the truth about who she was. Though Maybelle bragged about how important she was, Minnie knew she was barely tolerated among the better families in Denver. Margaret's mother had often told her not to pursue the acquaintance.

Even if Minnie shared the family she worked for, it might lead to questions. Questions she wasn't sure she should answer.

As they walked down the street, a gust of wind hit, pushing her into Hugh.

"Pardon me," she said, stepping away.

He smiled at her as he patted her arm. "It's no trouble. The wind is strong, and it couldn't be helped. Besides, we are to be married soon."

The dreaded marriage talk. He was a rather large man, not in a grotesque sort of way, but in the sense that she wondered if he would crush her to death on their wedding night. At least Lord Milliken was slight of build and didn't look like he had the strength to crush a fly. But clearly, he'd been strong enough to make Minnie fearful.

If only she could make friends with the other ladies, enough to get their advice. But it was such a personal topic that to become good enough friends to share such intimate details in such a short time seemed almost impossible.

"Not too soon, I hope? I thought we were to be given time to get to know one another."

He looked taken aback at her words. "Of course not," he said hastily. "But I did promise the Reverend that we'd make quick work of things."

Quick work of things? Like it was a simple task to be checked off the list?

"I see," she said, trying not to sound disappointed. "Will there be wine at our wedding?"

From the way he looked at her, she wished she hadn't

been so open in her question. But if she couldn't get advice on how to make the wedding night tolerable, she would have to take her mother's advice.

"I don't believe the saloon has wine, just spirits."

A lady never drank spirits, according to Margaret's mother. But perhaps if it were an emergency, such indiscretion could be excused. After all, her mother did put a nip of brandy in her tea when Margaret was ill. Surely one's wedding night could also be an exception.

"I see. Do you indulge in spirits? Is that what we shall toast with?"

He looked at her as if she had asked an extremely improper question. "Why are you so curious about the drink?"

Most young ladies wouldn't ask these questions, but she wasn't asking as a young lady. What were maids supposed to talk about? She wasn't sure, because she had never been with Minnie and her peers. Only the two of them, and they generally talked of things of interest to Margaret. She'd thought those were also Minnie's interests, but none of the women here seemed to talk about any of the things familiar to Margaret. She'd asked Birdie, the seamstress, about her embroidery, but the woman had been too focused on getting her cloth in order. Perhaps in time, when they were settled, they could spend an afternoon working on a sampler.

Hugh was still looking at her as if he expected an answer.

"I heard that was a way of life in towns like these," she said. "I'm just trying to see what I should expect."

He wore the same look of disgust that seemed to be permanently present when they were together. The whole point in Minnie coming here was for him to have someone as a helper, not someone who was obviously such a burden. Why had she thought she could so easily take her maid's place?

Then he gave a long-suffering sigh. "I'm sure there are many tales about the lawlessness and drunken antics in mining towns. However, Sheriff Draven runs a tight ship, and you needn't worry about those things in Noelle."

His expression softened, and for a moment she thought she might have detected a hint of kindness in it. "If you are worried about my own proclivities, I can assure that while I do indulge occasionally, I've never been prone to drunkenness."

A question she hadn't considered. But she was grateful for the answer.

"Thank you. I find that reassuring."

Except she wasn't entirely reassured. True, she wouldn't have to fear him having too much drink, but would there be something to numb the horrible experience that was to come?

He led her across the street to one of the nearby buildings. While Noelle lacked proper sidewalks, someone had at least shoveled the snow to create a path and spread ashes to keep people from slipping as they walked. Her mother had often looked down upon households that didn't have proper porches and walkways, and were therefore forced to use even more ashes to make the way clear. However, Margaret was grateful Hugh had been so thoughtful for her safety.

The building appeared to be well-built, with a neat sign that said, "Assayer."

He led her through the door, and she was pleased by the tidy appearance of the shop. While she couldn't say what any of the items were used for, everything seemed to have its place. Dominating the room was a rather large stove-looking apparatus. The fire was burning, and Hugh immediately went over to put more wood in it.

"I like to keep the fire hot, in case Charlie brings me

something to examine. I have to heat the ore to separate it into the various metals and measure their properties."

She had absolutely no idea why he'd need a fire to do so, but she smiled pleasantly. "Well, I know I will never be cold then."

"Indeed not. I hope you won't be too warm, but we do have windows that open, just in case." He smiled at her, almost indulgently. "You see, we aren't entirely devoid of luxuries. Even though it was a tremendous expense, I see it as a good investment for comfort. During busy times, it gets quite hot in here, so I hope it will make your life here more bearable."

His words were meant to show his hospitality, but they only made her feel more uncomfortable.

"Bearable?" she asked. "You make it sound quite like a prison. Are you trying to talk me out of marrying you? If you don't wish to marry me, you should just say so."

At least he had the courtesy to look embarrassed. "No!" He shook his head. "Not at all. That is, I do wish to marry you. I'm an honorable man. I keep my word. I just..."

Hugh let out a long sigh. "I will admit that when I thought I was marrying a maid, I assumed she would be used to a more difficult life. Knowing that you come from a more... sheltered background, I was hoping to reassure you that there are some comforts here."

She gave a slight nod to indicate she acknowledged his words, but she couldn't find appropriate speech to give an answer. He might say he wanted her, but his every action made her think he'd just as soon have her get on the next wagon out of town.

SHE WAS TOO IMPERTINENT. Hugh wasn't a betting man, but

he'd wager his entire savings on the fact that Minnie Gold was not who she said she was. A maid, even one no longer employed, would not speak so directly or boldly. Not that he expected her to bow to him and polish his boots, but her demeanor lacked a humbleness that spoke of a more elevated station than she claimed to have come from. Even his mother's ladies' maid, who had been a gentleman's by-blow, wouldn't have questioned his intentions.

Would he still marry Minnie? As he'd told her, he'd given his word as a man of honor. Did he like it? Not one bit. Of all the things he could not abide, it was a liar.

Which, of course, made him a hypocrite in a sense. Hugh was well-aware that he'd been hiding his own identity. Though he'd never lied, sometimes it felt like a lie, denying his birthright. But it wasn't as though he'd ever inherit, or that there was any future for him back in England. And, he'd never pretended to be anyone he was not.

But Minnie?

He watched as she ran a gloved finger over his desk, like she was inspecting it. Maid, his foot. She was no more a maid than he'd been a stable boy.

The question was, who was she really, and why had she lied? He could only assume she was running from something. But what? An abusive father or husband? A crime? Perhaps he should have a word with Sheriff Draven to use his skills to look into this Minnie Gold, or whoever she was.

Then he let out a long sigh. Reverend Chase Hammond was counting on them all to get married. However, it would also be a snag in Chase's plans to have one of the brides be a fugitive. Though a lot of people used towns like Noelle to hide from the law, that was not the sort of attention they wanted if the railroad was going to come through here. And, knowing what he knew about the ore Charlie kept bringing him, if Noelle was going to survive, they had to get the railroad to stop here. There would be nothing else to keep the town alive. Charlie might be hoping for a new gold strike, but each day made it look more and more impossible.

Minnie looked at him expectantly. She'd heard his sigh and probably thought he'd meant to speak to her. Which he should be doing, instead of worrying about the fate of the town. With his skill, he could go almost anywhere and find work. But he liked Noelle, liked the feeling of being settled. Which meant he'd do what he could to court his intended and hope he wasn't making a terrible mistake.

"Would you like to see where you'll be living?" he asked, gesturing to the door that led to his quarters. They weren't much, as he'd told her, but it was a far sight better than what many in this town had. Hopefully, come spring, he'd have the means to build a house on the edge of town.

Minnie looked relieved, like she'd been trying to think of conversation and was lost for words. This awkwardness didn't bode well for their future together. Would they ever have anything to talk about? He'd always hated the strained silence in the drawing room between his parents. In coming to America, he'd hoped to avoid that fate for himself. And here he was, getting trapped in a marriage to save a town because it was the right thing to do.

He led her inside the small space. What fault would she find with it? He hadn't been able to tell from her inspection of his workspace if it had met with her approval. But as they entered the room, she took off her cloak, then her hat and gloves.

"This is a pleasant place," she said. "Very cozy."

As he took her belongings, he realized that he hadn't given enough thought to providing a wife enough space for her things. He'd need to add another hook by the door to hang her cloak. For now, he could put it over his own.

The living quarters had been enough for a bachelor. But with Minnie here, it felt like anything but.

She paused at the bed. He'd built it himself, allowing extra room for his height. The few people he'd allowed in here had always expressed surprise at how large it was, but Minnie was looking at it as though it, too, failed to meet her expectations.

Should he tell her he'd made it himself? Or would that lead to more of her disdain?

Fortunately, she didn't comment as she turned around, bringing her attention to the table and two chairs that dominated the other side.

"I see there are two chairs," she said.

"I made a second one as soon as I knew a wife was coming. I hope it's to your liking."

Minnie nodded. "I appreciate all the thought you've put into my arrival. Did you make all the furniture in this room? And the other?"

There didn't seem to be any disdain in her voice, only curiosity. Had he been too quick to judge her?

As she ran her fingers along the shelves he'd built for storage, she looked at him. "It's very fine work."

"Thank you," he said. "I did build most of it. With my height, it's important to me to have furniture to match."

He looked at her, noticing once again how very small she seemed. Was she strong enough for this life? He'd hoped that being a maid, she'd be more… sturdy.

"But don't worry," he added. "I have a stool I built for you to stand on so you can reach everything. And if there are other ways I can provide for your comfort, I will do my best. With so many of my evenings spent alone, I've had plenty of time to build things."

The furrow in her brow told him he'd once again said something to displease her.

"But your visits to..." Minnie hesitated. "The place I'm staying?"

This woman was such a troublesome creature. Most chose to ignore the existence of such places, or that men occasionally had cause to visit.

Her expectant expression told him he wasn't going to get away with not answering.

"If I'm up to socializing, I spend most of that time in the saloon. I'm not as familiar with *La Maison* as you seem to think."

"But... that girl? Angelique?"

Hadn't he already told Minnie he planned on being faithful to her? Though he'd admit if the rest of his marriage was as lacking in excitement as these past few hours with her, he'd need to spend time talking with Angelique, if only to have something to ease the boredom.

"She's a friend."

He'd been hasty in suggesting Minnie become friends with her, considering that even in a rough mining town, those two classes didn't intersect. But Angelique was a good person, as were a number of Madame's girls, and it was a shame more of the people in this town didn't see that. True, there were others he could do without, but that was the way of any town.

"I tried," Minnie said, her voice almost like that of a child's. "But she wouldn't even answer me when I said hello when I saw her later. It was extremely awkward."

So, no one had clued her in on Angelique's condition. "Angelique is mute. She can't speak."

"How am I supposed to be friends with someone who can't speak?"

He shrugged. "You talk to her like a regular person. She can listen just fine, and if you watch her body language and give her the opportunity to communicate in other ways, you'd be surprised at how much both of you get out of the conversation."

At least Minnie appeared to be considering his words. "All right then. I'll do my best. I'm not very good at socializing. With my work, there was never time."

She turned her attention to the cookstove in the corner, but rather than seeming pleased at the fine model, she looked almost terrified.

"You can't cook, can you?" he asked the question, even though he knew her answer.

Minnie let out a long sigh. "It wasn't part of my duties. But I'm willing to learn. I know you are disappointed by me, but I will do my best to become the woman you need. I only hope you're willing to be patient and kind in the process."

Had he been so harsh with her that she already feared him? Or was her fear more about the past she was running from?

"I suppose I am not the man you expected, either. Let us both be patient with one another as we build our new life together."

His words didn't ease the lines on her face. He hadn't thought much about what would induce her to marry a complete stranger. Hopefully, she would soon learn he was not the sort to mistreat a woman.

He started to gesture to the tiny loft above his living quarters that he used for storage, but he heard the door to his shop open. Hugh hoped it was Charlie, with news about the mine. So far, it didn't look promising that his friend would find a larger vein of gold. But it would be nice for Hugh to be wrong. Some men had too much pride to admit their faults. But not Hugh. If he were wrong in this, he would gladly say so.

However, when he entered the other room, the woman

standing in his workshop was a far bigger blow than if it had been Charlie telling him the gold was gone.

"Arabella. What are you doing here?"

His brother's wife took off her hat and gloves in the same manner Minnie had done, only Hugh couldn't help noticing how much finer Arabella's things were. The fur-lined cape might be better suited to the weather than Minnie's tattered cloak, but the finery seemed out of place.

"That's hardly an appropriate greeting for family," she said, handing him her belongings. "Now have your servant fetch me some tea so we can talk. I've had a long journey, and you can't imagine the difficulty I've had in reaching this godforsaken place."

Minnie entered the room. "Visitors. And she mentioned something about family? Am I to meet your family? This is very good news indeed."

No, this was not good news. This was the worst news of all.

"Again, I ask you, what are you doing here?" He was being rude, and he hated to do so in front of the bride he was already struggling to get to know. But there was no way he was going to allow Arabella to stay any longer than he had to.

"You wound me. But at least you have called for your maid." She turned to Minnie. "Now go fetch my tea. And some refreshment. Whatever you have on hand is fine. I'm famished after the terrible food I've suffered on my travels."

Minnie looked absolutely terrified by the request.

He glared at Arabella. "As always, you fail to know your place. You might outrank the both of us, but Minnie is no servant. She is my fiancée. And you will treat her with respect."

He looked over at Minnie to reassure her, to let her know that he would not tolerate such disrespect in his home.

Besides, they were in America now, and not obligated under the stuffy rules of inheritance and precedence.

"And you forget your place," she said. "As the wife of a duke, I outrank the son of one. Or I should say, the late duke."

Hugh had known of his father's death, of course. He still had friends who wrote him with news. He was glad his mother had been gone for some time now, as she would turn over in her grave to see Arabella as the new duchess. He'd always thought his mother's death had been brought on by despair of his brother's engagement to this woman.

"What do you mean, a duke's son?" Minnie asked.

Arabella gave a nasty little laugh. At one time he'd thought it charming, until he realized that the expression only came as a result of her finding herself in a position to be particularly nasty. He glared at Arabella before turning to Minnie.

"I came to America to start a new life, but it is true. My father was a duke. But as the third son, I have no chance at inheriting, and my brother John, her husband, has inherited my father's title and lands."

But where was John? For the first time, it struck him as being odd that he was not present.

"Where's my brother?" he asked.

"You have not heard?" Arabella sounded bored, like he'd asked her a ridiculous question.

"He is dead. Hunting accident. I'm surprised no one has told you, but I'm glad I could notify you in person."

John. Dead. Hugh took a step back, and if he were a woman, he might have needed a gentleman's assistance to sit in a more comfortable place. Minnie came beside him and put her arm around him.

"I am so sorry for your loss," she said.

Dear, sweet Minnie. The woman he barely knew offered him comfort in such a genuine way. It was a stark contrast to the emotionless expression on his sister-in-law's face. He knew, of course, that Arabella had loved John no more than Hugh loved Minnie. In many ways, it was a similar arrangement. She had married for the security of money and a title. John, however, had thought himself in love. And oh, how he had loved her. Unfortunately, his wife had never returned his affection. At least from the emotionless way she stood before Hugh now, he could assume she hadn't.

Perhaps Hugh had misjudged Minnie. Perhaps she would be a suitable mate after all.

Hugh could still remember the day Arabella told him she would be marrying John. Hugh had been the one courting her. He'd brought her home for a weekend to meet the family. It had never occurred to him that her ambitions lay more with the opportunity to spend time with his brother, who was a known recluse, preferring the company of his hounds and horses at the estate. But in the course of her visit, she had made it clear that her real target was John. And Hugh had been left in the cold.

After the wedding, Arabella had slipped into Hugh's room, confessing that he was the one she truly loved, that as a younger son he could not secure her future, so she'd been forced to marry John. He'd tried convincing her to make her marriage with John work. However, Arabella continued her pursuit of Hugh, so he left, pursuing his dream of coming to America.

He put his arm around Minnie. "Thank you for your consideration. It comforts me greatly to have you by my side during this time. John and I were quite close as boys, and I can hardly comprehend the tragedy."

He turned his gaze on Arabella. "How could this have happened? John was an excellent hunter. I can't imagine any sort of accident befalling him."

She gave a casual shrug as if it were a trivial thing, the death of her husband, and Hugh's brother.

"I cannot say. I know nothing of such matters. All I know is that I'm finally free. We are finally free. All these years of longing and wishing to be together. Hugh, our time is now."

Minnie made a choking noise and he pulled her closer to him. "You're too late. Minnie and I are to be married, and I'm quite certain we will suit well together."

"Suit well together?" Arabella gave a toss of her head. "That is what I said about marrying John. And look where that got me. A widow in my prime, with two young sons. But at least now, you can come home and take your rightful place at the estate."

That would never happen. In his time in America, he'd discovered that he quite enjoyed being here. He liked not having people scrape and bow. He hated the artifice and the way being a lord seemed to sway people's opinion of him. And then, of course, soon as they found out that he was the third son, dismissed him. He would never inherit, not without tragedy befalling the family, and that was something he'd always fervently prayed against. He did not wish his brothers ill, even when Arabella had chosen John. As far as he was concerned, he was well rid of a woman whose affections were more about the size of a man's estate than the size of a man's heart.

"I'm afraid you've wasted your time. I have no intention of returning to England. There is nothing left there to entice me." Then he smiled down at Minnie. "My life is here with my business and my future bride."

Minnie made a noise, like she didn't quite agree with his words. It must be a shock to her, finding out about his background in this way. He'd always intended telling her at some point, but he hadn't figured out when or how. No one in Noelle knew he was a lord. And he hadn't wanted them to.

He liked that they all knew him as merely a man. A man with a reputation for being honest and, he hoped, a good person.

"But you must. You can inherit now."

The earnest look on Arabella's face made him sick. He didn't want to inherit. He had spent his entire life knowing that there was not a single chance that he would ever become the duke. And frankly, he'd rather enjoyed it. It had allowed him to study his passions and learn about metallurgy. He'd built his own workshop on the estate, where he'd been able to study various metals and materials to find out what they were made of. It had been fascinating to him and, although he hadn't known it at the time, it had given him the opportunity to learn a valuable trade that provided him a very good living in America.

"As I have told you, I have no intention of ever returning to England. As for becoming duke, you have two sons, and then there is Gerald, my middle brother. One of them shall inherit."

Rather than acknowledging the simple logic he had just presented to her, Arabella looked furious.

"Young John is a sickly boy. I can't imagine he will grow up to take on the duke's responsibilities, even though he technically holds the title. Charles is still a baby, and as you know, things happen to children. As for Gerald, he is a complete idiot. He doesn't deserve to inherit. He can't run an estate, manage finances, or do anything a duke would."

The sickening feeling gnawing at Hugh's stomach made it almost impossible to stand. But he squared his shoulders and glared at Arabella.

"I'm sorry to hear that your boys are unwell. Perhaps, rather than trying to find substitutes for them, you should be with them, mothering them, enjoying what time you have, and, dare I say it, finding ways of improving their health. As for Gerald, he is a good man, and I've always thought he would make an excellent duke."

Her face glowed hotter than his furnace when he was working metal. "Do you not understand? This is your opportunity."

Had she been so callous and cold when he'd first fallen in love with her? He couldn't imagine having ever loved a woman like this. He looked at Minnie, who stood silently beside him, taking in all this information. What must she think of the family she was marrying into?

"I have never wanted to be duke. I don't know how you ever got that idea in your head. I will not inherit, and I will not return to England. Focus your attention on molding your sons into men who can lead with kindness, goodness, and justice. That is what the world needs. That is what the estate and its people need."

None of those values were high on Arabella's list, but given the almost murderous way she looked at him, he wasn't going to give her any encouragement. Why she thought he would be willing to go along with whatever ridiculous scheme she'd concocted, he didn't know. But he was grateful to have Minnie by his side to strengthen him.

Though he'd begun the day with doubts about her, Hugh's only regret was that they weren't already married. At least then he could send Arabella on her way and end her meddling once and for all. Now, he needed to find a way to get her to leave, and soon.

CHAPTER 3

THE SECOND DAY OF CHRISTMAS

DECEMBER 26, 1876

Because there were no hotels in Noelle, they had been forced to house Arabella with the other ladies at *La Maison*. Hugh had point blank told her that there was no place for her in his home, and for that, Minnie was glad. What an unexpected twist to be running from one titled marriage into another one. The difference was, with Hugh, there'd be no balls, no fancy carriages, and no expectation for Minnie to be a woman of society. Hugh had even asked both her and Arabella to remain quiet about his true identity. Something that eased Margaret's guilt about who she really was. If only she didn't have to share a room with the insufferable Arabella. Minnie had done her best to avoid the other woman.

But now, as they finished breakfast and were now

retreating to the parlor, Minnie couldn't help feeling like none of this was going to be as easy as she hoped.

And she was right.

Arabella entered the room, looking as disdainful and bored as she had when she arrived the day before.

"Waiting for Hugh?" she asked, sounding smug. "It's not uncommon for a man to have second thoughts on his wedding day. Men like him need a certain type of wife, and a woman like you cannot possibly understand his needs."

She gave a hideous laugh. Granted, Minnie was no lady, but Margaret did come from one of the wealthiest families in America. Maybe not all of America, but when her father spoke, people listened.

When the ladies were seated with their tea, Arabella pulled out her bag and removed out a very nice sampler that she'd been working on. Of course, the other woman would have it with her. No lady traveled without.

"Minnie," she said. "do go and find me a stand upon which I can finish my work. I realize there most likely isn't proper equipment, but surely you can find something. It's a task you must have often done for your mistress."

She tried not to groan. Arabella was so intent on keeping her in her place, even though Hugh had made it clear he would be marrying her today. But at least, once the ceremony had been completed she would be able to go to his house and stay there.

"There isn't anything, I'm afraid. I, too, enjoy embroidery. But alas, there are no supplies. What you have with you will have to do."

Arabella looked at her as though she were a complete idiot, like she hadn't expected an answer. Which was silly, considering Minnie and Margaret had often done embroidery together. It was a pleasant way to spend the afternoon, especially when none of the people her mother deemed suitable were available for entertainment.

"Really? Your employer must've been extremely indulgent," she said, looking thoughtful. "The family you worked for must've been of some means, allowing you such a pastime. I find most servants are simply too busy to indulge in such diversions."

Minnie let out a long sigh. She'd forgotten that the other woman didn't know the story she'd told everybody upon arrival. "I worked for a wealthy family in Denver as a companion to the daughter. Her mother was most particular about the company she kept, and I acted as a chaperone. She appreciated passing the time with someone who shared her hobbies and skills. Therefore, I learned along with her. I enjoyed many of the entertainments of a young lady."

Arabella made a sympathetic noise. "It does seem strange, leaving such good circumstances to come to such a low place to marry a complete stranger? You must've done something terrible."

Minnie's face heated as she realized that suddenly, everyone was staring at her. Before she could come up with an answer, Hugh entered the room. At least his presence would keep her from facing this woman's ridicule. He wouldn't tolerate it, and perhaps it would make him move up the time of the wedding so that they could-

Minnie closed her eyes. Her wedding night would be tonight. She still hadn't determined what she was going to do about the humiliation. But surely it couldn't be worse than having this woman picking at her in front of everyone.

Finally, Minnie stood. At least that's how she thought she was supposed to behave around a duke. Or a duke's son. Her mother had tried explaining to her the proprieties of how to act around people with titles, and she still wasn't sure. Even though he'd asked them not to tell everyone that he was the son of a duke, it was still difficult not treating him as such.

"Good morning, Hugh," she said.

Arabella snickered, like Minnie had done something wrong. But either Hugh didn't notice, or he was too much of a gentleman to point it out. He walked up to her and greeted her warmly.

"Good morning. It's a fine day for our wedding, isn't it?"

Oh, how she wished she could rub Arabella's smug nose in those words. But it was enough that she'd witnessed them.

"Indeed, it is. I couldn't be prouder to marry you on such a day."

He escorted her back to where she had been sitting, then sat in a nearby chair. "The Reverend will be by soon. I told him we didn't need much fuss, but of course, I thought I should check with you to see if other arrangements should be made."

Anything to get out this horrible place with these horrible women. "I believe your plans will suit me just fine."

He smiled, and it warmed her in a funny way. It felt good to be looked upon with such affection, or maybe it was approval. She wasn't sure. But it didn't matter. It demonstrated that her prayer for a kind man had been answered.

"Minnie was just telling us about the family she came from," Arabella said.

"No, I wasn't," Minnie said. "They are of little import to any of you, and I prefer to respect their privacy."

"Or you have something to hide," Arabella said. "As a representative of the Duke of Hallstead, I'm not sure I can allow Hugh to go along with this farce if we don't at least know where his bride comes from."

The woman was impossible. And yet, it was clear she wouldn't rest without an answer. Minnie had never been good at lying, and the lies she'd already told weighed heavily upon her.

She took a deep breath. "I've done nothing wrong. I do not wish to increase my status by using a family who has treated me so well. They're good people, and my time with them was quite enjoyable.

"If it was so enjoyable, why did you leave?" Arabella's taunt made her uncomfortable in the face of the man she was to marry. Especially because others in the room were now listening to the conversation.

"It's no secret," she said. "My mistress was going to be married. Her future husband said there was no room for her to take her own staff. I'm sure I could have found another position, but I've always hoped to someday become a wife and mother. This seemed like the perfect opportunity."

Minnie had told this to the benevolent society. The other women in the room murmured as if they understood. And why wouldn't they? She'd been telling them that same story as well.

"Who knew that a servant would have such lofty aspirations?" Arabella said, snickering again.

Hugh cleared his throat. Minnie turned and looked at him, and he gave her another smile. "It's good for all of us to have dreams. It is the thing I love the most about being in America. A man could be born into any circumstances, and then he can make his life what he wants. I'm grateful you entrusted me with your future."

Her heart swelled, and once again, she was reassured that marrying him was the right thing to do.

"Aspirations are dangerous things," Arabella said. "Particularly when they involve a future duke. I must insist-"

"Arabella." He glared at her

She stood. "I will not have it. It is ludicrous that you are not using your title, Lord Hugh. You could be the next Duke of Hallstead. And we must know if the mother of the future dukes is worthy."

"Madame, you forget yourself. And you forget the sons you have borne. They are the rightful heirs to Hallstead. And if not them, then my brother Gerald. You are wasting your time. Given your complete lack of respect for my wishes in sharing our family business, I will allow you no say in any of this. Kindly refrain from speaking of it or harassing my future wife again."

Hugh looked like he was about to storm out, but then he stopped and looked at Minnie. "Is this how she's been treating you since her arrival?"

Minnie nodded. He returned to his seat. "Then I will remain with you, a faithful companion as you had been to your mistress."

A faithful companion. That was exactly what she had hoped for. What made her heart hurt every time she thought of her maid. She'd let Minnie go so Minnie could have happiness, only Minnie had found death.

Arabella gave an exaggerated huff as she returned to her chair. "I still think we should be concerned about her lack of background. If she has nothing to hide, then she'd tell us who she worked for. You'd do well to have the sheriff make sure she's not wanted by the law."

Minnie remained silent, but one of the other girls looked at her suspiciously. Would these women, who Minnie wanted so desperately to befriend, also fear her? As more glances came her way, Minnie felt that she owed it to the people she'd be sharing this town with.

"I worked for the Coveney family. I refuse to gossip about them, as they were good people, and I will not give them cause to think ill of me."

Arabella's eyes widened.

"Coveney? As in Coveney Coal?"

With Coveney Coal stamped on so many signs, she couldn't lie. "Yes."

She looked like she had dozens of questions, but Minnie shook her head. "As I have said, I will say no more on the family."

But that only made the lines on Arabella's face deepen. "Then there is indeed a problem."

She stood. "Someone should call for Sheriff Draven. Margaret Coveney, Minnie's so-called mistress, is missing. There are notices everywhere. The family is quite desperate for news of her. I'm sure he would like to question anyone who claims to know the daughter. Who knows, you might have even had a hand in it."

Margaret sank back against the chair, and closed her eyes, wanting to be sick. She should have known her parents would search for her. She left her mother a note that she'd paid a newspaper boy to deliver. She expected that perhaps her father would have investigators look for her, but she hadn't expected them to make a big fuss. Too much embarrassment.

Opening her eyes, Minnie said, "I've done nothing wrong."

But even Hugh looked at her like he expected her to go to the sheriff and tell him what she knew of Margaret's disappearance.

Arabella got up and walked over to her. "It was all over the papers. The Coveney heiress is missing, and her maid was found dead. So, you are either lying about being the Coveney's maid, or you are Margaret Coveney."

Then she gave a satisfied smile. "And I believe, given that your manners are too fine to be a maid's, but not fine enough to be a duchess's, you are really Margaret Coveney."

Minnie's insides churned. It had already been so difficult,

living a lie. But now what was she to do with her lie exposed? Was it finally time to tell the truth?

She looked over to Hugh, hoping that he would be sympathetic, considering he, too, had hidden his true identity.

ARABELLA'S WORDS were almost inconceivable. Hugh couldn't imagine Minnie hurting anyone, let alone killing anyone. And while she could have easily lied about working for the Coveney family, that had been one of the truest things he had sensed from her. If she was Margaret Coveney, it only made sense why he had thought she was better than she said she was. It would account for her inconsistencies.

He looked at Minnie. "Are you really Margaret Coveney?"

As Minnie nodded, tears ran down her cheeks.

Though he was grateful she had admitted the truth, part of Hugh felt ill. He couldn't marry a young lady whose parents thought she was missing, especially not the heiress to Coveney Coal. Everyone in Colorado knew Arthur Coveney was a shrewd businessman who wanted nothing but the best for his family. The real Minnie probably had been every bit as sheltered as Margaret had claimed. When he'd first come to Denver, he'd heard about the Coveney heiress and how nothing other than a lord would do. Hugh might have the courtesy title, but he didn't have the official title Coveney would require for his daughter.

"We must notify your father that you're safe," he said. Then he stood. "I need to talk to Sheriff Draven, and then I will stop by the telegraph office to let Margaret's father about his daughter."

Hugh wanted to be sick. Not only had he almost married an heiress, but Arthur Coveney was an extremely powerful man whose ire would be enough to destroy Noelle. It would be very easy for Arthur to influence the railroad's decision to come to Noelle. More importantly, if he was angry enough, he could refuse to supply the railroad with coal should they come to Noelle against his wishes.

Minnie, no, Margaret, stood. "Please tell me we're still getting married."

He turned and looked at her. "I'm sorry. I'm not sure I can answer that. I need to speak to your father. It was a foolhardy thing you did, coming here. Your family must be incredibly worried."

Margaret squared her shoulders. "They're only worried because my mother's dream of my being Lady Whatever has been dashed. They have plans to marry me off to a horrible man, Lord Milliken. I can't do it. He did something terrible to Minnie that made her afraid. She told me she was a coward because she wouldn't be able to accompany me once I was married to him. So, I helped her get a place here with Benevolent Lambs, only she was killed in a carriage accident en route. I got to her side as she was dying, and she begged me to take her place."

Tears streamed down Margaret's face as she looked at him. "Please, I beg of you. Marry me. Minnie told me that she prayed every day that I would find a way out because Lord Milliken was so horrible. I don't know what he did to her, but she said it was unspeakable."

The fear in Margaret's voice was real. And though Hugh had never met the man, he had heard of him. Back in England, Milliken had gambled away his family's estate, and it was well known that the man needed a wealthy bride. Somehow, in the intervening years, he'd become so desperate as to seek a wealthy American heiress.

How much of Margaret's words were the truth, and how

much an exaggeration? He'd already known he couldn't trust her. Now, he was even more uncertain.

"You are engaged?" Mrs. Walters stared at Margaret.

Margaret nodded slowly.

Though engaged wasn't married, it might as well be, with the various contracts that had to have been signed. As Hugh looked at Mrs. Walters, he knew she must be thinking of the consequences, as well.

Mrs. Walters shook her head. "The Benevolent Society of Lost Lambs exists to help women in trouble, but we have no precedent for women who are already married or engaged. But you fear him, you say?"

"Minnie was terrified of him, and even though she refused to give me details, I knew it was for good reason. We were close enough that I didn't need them. Something about the way he looked at me frightened me. We found a way out for Minnie, and it wasn't until I lost her that there was one for me."

More tears streamed down her face, and Hugh knew Margaret was telling the truth. But even here in America, where people had greater freedom than in England, one didn't just take a young woman from her family and marry her when she was already promised to another.

She turned to him again. "Please. You must help me."

What was he supposed to do?

Mrs. Walters murmured softly, like she was praying under her breath, then looked up at Margaret. "I'll see what I can do. No one should be forced into an unwanted marriage."

Though Hugh agreed, he also knew that it was easier said than done, considering Margaret's father was one of the most powerful men in this part of the country.

He could feel Arabella's eyes upon him. And when he turned to her, the knowing look she gave him made the sick feeling in his stomach worse. She thought she'd won. Without a bride, he was more vulnerable to whatever plot she was hatching.

But what was her plan?

"I see I have preserved the family once more," Arabella said, looking entirely too satisfied with herself. "Now there is no reason for us to not marry. It is as if Fate herself has stepped down to offer a blessing upon our union. The family will grow and prosper through us, and we will someday look at this little escapade and laugh."

He glared at her. "You are forgetting your sons and my brother. They will inherit before me."

"As I have said, these are things easily handled."

He shook his head. "Not in the way you are implying."

He would have to look into things back home, and caution his brother about Arabella's visit, and her wicked plans. Such a woman did not deserve to play a role in the family's future. But first, he needed to have a word with Draven and Charlie. They needed to figure out what to do about Margaret. As for Arabella, he could also use help containing the situation.

As he left the building, he spotted Charlie headed for the assayer's office.

"Charlie! Walk with me to see Draven."

He stopped. "I was on my way to see you. The men found some new ore I'd like you to take a look at."

Hopefully something promising. The ore had been looking rather thin lately, and Charlie had had to lay off some of his miners. Charlie might not want to admit it, but he seemed to genuinely care for his men. With the bad news Hugh was going to have to deliver, they could use something positive.

"I'll be eager to examine it. First, we have more urgent business."

On the way to the sheriff's office, they ran into Draven. "Is it time for the wedding?"

Hugh shook his head. "Unfortunately, there isn't going to be a wedding. Not today. Maybe not ever. I've just discovered that Minnie isn't who she says she is."

Charlie stared at him blankly. "Is anyone who they say they are?" he asked, looking at Hugh, then at Draven, then back to Hugh.

Draven shook his head. "I hear you're some kind of lord. I hope we're not supposed to bow to you now that your secret is out. I guess our jokes about your lordship weren't far off the mark."

Hugh groaned. This was exactly why he hadn't wanted anyone to know who he really was. "I never lied," he said. "But that's not the point. Minnie is really Margaret Coveney, daughter of-"

"Not Arthur Coveney?" Charlie said, sounding more discouraged than surprised.

"The one and only. How did you come up with his name so quickly?"

"I got a wire about a missing girl. I meant to bring it up to Draven, but I must have forgotten."

Charlie relayed the details of the report he'd gotten, and Hugh nodded. "That sounds like the story Arabella told." He then shared what Minnie had told him.

"I've heard of Lord Milliken," Charlie said. "He's come to Colorado on hunting trips. There are stories about what he's done on those trips. Terrible things. I pity the woman forced to marry him. She'd be better off marrying you."

The three men went to the telegraph office, where they sent messages to their respective contacts. The first message went to Arthur Coveney, who responded almost immediately. He had men nearby, and they would come for Margaret. It saddened Hugh to hear that the man's response conveyed more annoyance than concern. Of course, one couldn't discern a man's tone in a telegraph message, so perhaps Hugh was reading too much into it. But shouldn't the father ask how his daughter was? Surely a rich man could afford the expense of those few lines. He'd actually referred to Margaret as his property. No wonder Margaret had been so eager to leave.

When he showed the messages to Charlie, he shrugged. "I'm not surprised. It follows what I've heard about the man."

Something about Charlie's attitude made him even more fearful for Margaret.

"What do we do, then?" Hugh asked. "You've already admitted that Margaret will be marrying a terrible man. And her father doesn't seem to care. How do we help her?"

Charlie shook his head. "I don't know. Arthur Coveney is a terrible man to cross. His vindictiveness is well-documented in the papers. He would ruin us all, and Margaret would still be marrying Lord Milliken. I'm not sure how to keep her here without putting the town at risk."

Reverend Chase Hammond entered the telegraph office. "I hear there is a problem with one of the brides and the wedding."

Hugh filled him in, and as soon as he mentioned the Coveney name, Chase's eyes widened.

"Not Arthur Coveney's daughter."

At everyone's automatic response, Hugh wondered how Margaret could have thought she was going to get away with her plan. Had she actually thought that her father would let her go so easily? And that when her father did find her, what had she thought he would do when he discovered her married to someone not of his choosing?

The Reverend looked at Hugh. "It's well-known that Coveney will settle for no less than a lord to marry his daughter."

All eyes turned to Hugh. Draven spoke first.

"If you're a duke's son, doesn't that make you a lord? You might still be able to marry Margaret after all."

The other men chuckled and gave mock bows, calling him Lord Hugh.

"That's precisely why I left England," Hugh said. "My title is a courtesy title. I'll never be duke, and my children will inherit nothing, which would do nothing to further Coveney's aspirations."

Charlie shrugged. "Perhaps we can find you someone else to marry. Or at least someone willing to say she's married to you when the railroad men are here, like Draven has."

With as much trouble as this bride was giving him, Hugh wasn't sure he wanted to try again. Especially because the reminder of why he refused to give his heart away was also in Noelle.

As if he was reading his thoughts, the Reverend looked over at Hugh. "What about the woman who came looking for you? Arabella? Is she willing to stay here? Could she marry you?"

Hugh stared at him. "I'd sooner marry Madame Bonheur. Arabella is up to no good, and we should all be on our guard against her. I've sent messages to my contacts, hoping for more information about her plans."

The men all nodded, but his warning didn't solve their problem of what to do about another bride. Margaret would go home, and they would have to find another way to save Noelle.

Even though Hugh had found Minnie, rather Margaret, difficult at first, he had to admit she'd grown on him. She had seemed eager to learn about her new life. Her willingness to fit into this new world, even though she was so unsuited to it, made her the perfect addition to the town. He was so angry with her for lying to him, but he had to admit to a soft spot in his heart for her being willing to give up her pampered life for a life such as this. He'd done the same, and he knew how difficult it was.

Maybe Margaret wasn't perfect, but the more Hugh was faced with the idea of letting her go, he wasn't sure he wanted to.

CHAPTER 4

THE THIRD DAY OF CHRISTMAS

DECEMBER 27TH, 1876

Since yesterday's big reveal, Minnie thought she'd noticed some of the women looking at her with sympathy. As she entered the kitchen for breakfast, the women seated at the table stopped their chatter. Penny, one of the brides she didn't know very well, turned to her. As she did so, she knocked over a pitcher of milk.

Penny jumped up. "Oh dear. I'm so sorry. I only meant to welcome you, because I imagine you feel terrible after yesterday's events. And now look at the mess I've made."

The other ladies had begun mopping up the spill, so she stepped forward and embraced Penny. "It's only milk, easily cleaned. Thank you for thinking of me. I can't tell you what it means to be accepted after revealing my secret."

Penny smiled at her. "We all have our secrets, and I

imagine that if you're running away from a forced marriage, the man must be terrible."

Sympathetic murmurs sounded throughout the room, as if they understood, and Minnie felt some of the shame at her lies fall away.

Cara, another bride, gave her an encouraging look. "A woman must always trust her instincts, especially when it comes to men. You did well to come here. So then, are we to call you Margaret?"

She thought about the question, and how difficult it had been to assume another identity. But she didn't feel like Margaret anymore. Nor did she want to be Margaret. Margaret would meekly go home and do exactly what her parents said. But for the moment of bravery Minnie had instilled in her, she would be absolutely miserable in her mother's parlor awaiting what felt like a death sentence. Minnie had been brave enough to follow her dreams, even though they didn't get her very far. She might have only been playing the role for a week, but it was enough time to make her never want to go back to being the person she once was.

Suddenly, what she wanted to be more than anything—was Minnie.

"No. Though the real Minnie was killed in a carriage accident, Margaret also died that day. She no longer exists. That woman can be no more. I am choosing to live the life that Minnie set out to live, and therefore, I am, and will remain, Minnie."

Mrs. Walters, the matchmaker, nodded approvingly. "The society exists to give women a new start, and many choose a new name to go with it. I can't imagine the courage it must have taken to leave your life behind, and we'll do all we can to support you here in Noelle."

This approval wasn't the same as what she'd sought when

chasing after her parents, begging for their affection. No, she was a strong woman, standing on her own two feet, surrounded by friends who supported her. To think she'd thought the other women would be unsympathetic. But as she looked at all the faces of the ladies at breakfast, she was glad they knew the truth.

If only Hugh were here to be part of this discussion. She'd like to think that he would understand. All her life, she'd done exactly what she was told, following everyone else's wishes. But what she wanted? Now that she'd been in Noelle for a while, she found she quite liked the place. She wanted to stay.

With its tiny shops and people who seemed to be friendlier and more accepting than she'd known in Denver, Noelle seemed like the perfect place to live.

The women finished their breakfast and went their separate ways, so she got herself some tea and biscuits to take to the parlor. She needed quiet time while she figured out a way to convince Hugh to let her stay. Just as she was making herself comfortable, Arabella came downstairs.

"Why didn't the servant bring me my breakfast?"

It was the same discussion they'd had the previous day, and yet Arabella seemed unable to comprehend the situation.

"This isn't England," Minnie said, smiling. "You can get your breakfast yourself. But I have fresh biscuits and tea, and I'm happy to share."

Arabella glared at her. As Minnie looked at the tiny woman, who seemed too small to carry all the rage that resided within her, she felt more pity than anger at her demanding ways.

It wasn't her job to wait on her, and when Margaret had servants, she never treated them with such contempt. Her mother used to tell her that even servants were people and they deserved kindness. But none of that had translated into being allowed friendship, and certainly she could see where she could have been kinder. But at least she treated people better than Arabella did.

Arabella came over, and Minnie poured her some tea. "Here you are," she said, handing the tea to her. "Would you like a biscuit?"

"That's not a biscuit," she said, practically snarling.

"I understand the biscuits in England are different, but you should try these. They're quite good."

Arabella made a noise, but she took one. "I do not like any of the things here in America. You people are completely ignorant of civilized ways."

She was just as much of a snob as Maybelle. Perhaps even worse. She knew she had better breeding than everyone else, whereas Maybelle just thought it. "I suppose you'll be returning to England as quickly as possible."

Arabella shook her head. "I will not return without Hugh. The family needs him."

Minnie didn't understand the woman's insistence on such a thing when he had clearly told her there was no way he would be returning home.

"But you must miss your sons," Minnie said, smiling at the woman. "Tell me about them."

Once again, Arabella made a noise like such a thing was beneath her. "They are well enough I suppose. I've never liked children, but as a duchess, it was my duty to produce children to inherit, which I did. They spend their time in the nursery with the maid."

That didn't sound like any way to live, or childhood. Exactly what things would be like if she married Lord Milliken. More and more, that kind of life seemed completely unlike what Margaret wanted for herself. Spending time with Kezia and baby Jem, she could see what the true bond between a mother and a child looked like. Margaret wasn't willing to settle for anything less. Not anymore. Now more than ever, the prospect of marrying Lord Milliken was intolerable.

Hugh wasn't perfect, but at least he treated her with respect. He treated everyone with respect. And they shared ideas on what family and life should look like.

Before Minnie was forced to think of something else to say to be polite to Arabella, Hugh entered the room.

"Good morning Miss Margaret," he said. "I trust you slept well."

He hadn't asked her how she'd slept until now, but there was a difference in how he held himself that told her things had changed between them. This wasn't a social call, even if he sounded friendly.

"I did, thank you," she said. "I hope today we can proceed with our wedding plans."

It was a bold statement, almost too bold for Margaret, but she was tiring of everyone telling her what they wanted for her, and what was best for her. No one asked her what she wanted. But she would stand by her earlier proclamation to the ladies. She had accepted Minnie's life, and the bravery that went with it.

"I'm sorry. I must not have made that clear. We will not be marrying. I've notified your father, and he has men on their way. They should be here soon. Perhaps in the next day or so."

"He's sending his men?" Was it wrong to be disappointed that he wasn't coming himself? Her mother wouldn't be up to the trip, but surely her father would want to see her. But, she supposed, that was how it always was with him. He was more interested in business, and how his daughter could be used to his advantage. He was probably relieved only that her absence was no longer a distraction.

"Yes. Apparently, he has men nearby."

How had she been so foolish as to think that she'd get

away with this? Her father knew everything, knew everyone, and it seemed no secret could be kept from him. Which meant whatever awful thing Minnie feared from Lord Milliken, her father knew. And approved. Margaret trusted Minnie's opinion far more than her father's, and it was sad to think that he was more interested in whatever advantage he'd gain from the match than her happiness.

Part of her wanted to be angry with Hugh for contacting him. But the more she thought about how her father had to have already known about Lord Milliken, and had men on their way, the more she realized that her only hope of escaping the carefully scripted life that had been laid out for her was marrying Hugh.

Could she convince him to change his mind?

She straightened, fully embodying the woman she wished to be. "As I told the ladies this morning, Margaret is no more. I'm choosing to live the life Minnie encouraged me to lead. I do not wish to go back to my father. I would like to continue with our wedding. My future is here."

"Unfortunately," he said, looking more serious than he'd looked before. "I stand by my earlier decision. There will be no wedding, not between us."

"I knew you'd listen to reason," Arabella said, standing. "Now we can leave this horrible place and finally live the lives we were meant to. I'm certain I saw a rat in our room last night."

He shook his head. "I also meant what I said about never marrying you. You'd best move on, because as soon as all the weddings take place, the original occupants of this house will return here, and they won't be kindly disposed to your continued presence. We promised them their stay in the saloon was temporary."

Minnie couldn't help feeling relieved. If there was no chance for Arabella, perhaps there was some chance for her.

Then Hugh turned his attention back to Minnie. "I thought, while we wait for your father's man, I'd give you a better tour of our town."

Perhaps, on the tour, she could get Hugh to see that they could still be married.

"Well, then," Minnie said, giving him her most charming smile. "I would be delighted to explore the town with you in the meantime."

"I'll just get my wrap," Arabella said.

Hugh turned to her. "No, you won't. You aren't invited. You should be planning your trip home."

Arabella brought her attention to Minnie and smirked. "A young lady needs a chaperone. I'd hate for her father to think she did without in this ungodly place."

Minnie glared back at her. "Technically, I'm already ruined. By Hugh. I have already spent time alone with him in his bedroom."

Her answer clearly didn't please him, who groaned. "It was my house, not my bedroom. Nothing untoward happened."

"But I did see the bed you made for yourself." She smiled at Arabella, then at Hugh. "I agree that you were the perfect gentleman. I'm just pointing out that it's a little too late for a chaperone to preserve my reputation. If you don't mind, I'm ready to leave for my tour- without Arabella."

The annoyed expression didn't leave his face, but he nodded. "I agree."

He held out his arm, and she felt slightly victorious at the gesture. If only Minnie were here to giggle with her about how she'd won the battle against Arabella. The wicked woman would still likely try to get between them, but at least for now, she had him all to herself.

When they stepped out into the cold winter air, she drew

in a breath. Though it stung her lungs, it was oddly refreshing after being in that stifling place.

As they walked down the path, he asked, "Will you really be ruined?"

"You know etiquette as well as I, perhaps even better, *Lord* Hugh. I've been staying in a brothel. I can only imagine the fit of vapors my mother is going to have when she finds out."

She gave a tiny laugh as she looked at him. No, he was not amused, and she wouldn't be either, at least when her mother started in on her. But for now, it felt good to laugh about a most intolerable situation.

"I do, and I'm sorry. I hope your fortune is enough of an inducement for your fiancé to continue with your marriage."

"I don't," she said, stopping to stare at him. "He is a terrible man. All the servants feared him, and Minnie told me all the maids did their best to avoid him because of the... liberties... he took."

She closed her eyes. Minnie especially had a reason to fear him, and though she'd never told her the details of what had transpired, it had made her fear him even more. And now, after spending time in a house of ill repute and hearing some of the bawdy things the women said in the saloon, she was certain that he had forced himself upon her maid. No wonder Minnie had feared him so much that she'd chosen to run away to be married rather than go off to England with Margaret and her new husband.

Hugh's voice interrupted her thoughts. "You fear him?"

She opened her eyes and looked at him. "Why else would I flee from society's most anticipated match? I overheard Mother telling my aunt Violet that the earl's pockets are let, and he must marry great wealth to survive."

Her stomach ached as she remembered the women's laughter. "Of course, they were rather pleased with themselves over the idea that I was marrying an earl, so they saw it as a good thing, but I found it revolting that they made light of such things. Supposedly, it's illegal to buy or sell a human being, but isn't that what men like my father are doing with their daughters?"

She and Minnie had spoken of this often, but when she'd mentioned it to her mother, she'd said it was a ridiculous notion and that clearly Margaret had been reading too many books.

"It's why I left England," Hugh said quietly. "You heard of my past with Arabella. The only thing that matters to her is status and money. She's already married as high as a woman in her circle can attain, and it's not likely another duke will offer for her. Which leaves me. But I will have no part of her plans."

He sounded as disappointed with his lot in life as she was with hers. Could he understand the similarity?

"So how can you think that sending me back to my father is the right thing?" she asked, looking at him as earnestly as she could.

But the expression on his face gave her no hope. "Because there is more at stake than our individual happiness."

Hugh gestured around him. "Noelle is dying, and we desperately need the railroad to come here to save it. This is the reason we need wives- to show that Noelle is a respectable town, and convince the railroad that people will come here."

Then he turned his gaze back on her. "That's why I'm showing you around, hoping you'll tell your father what a wonderful place this is, and he won't be so angry with us for harboring you. With his coal interests, a single word to the railroad would ruin us all."

So even Hugh was using her.

She'd known, of course, that theirs was to be a marriage of convenience, and even that they were trying to save the town. But this attempt at friendship and conversation was all about Margaret Coveney's influence.

"He doesn't listen to me. Why do you think he's marrying me off to an odious troll?"

Hugh nodded. "But if he knows we didn't intentionally take his daughter, and that we treated you well, surely he won't retaliate."

Retaliate. It was a word she hadn't considered, but everyone knew that no one crossed Arthur Coveney. Would he view this as an act of aggression?

Hugh wasn't going to marry her. She could see it clearly now, the set to his jaw, and his determination to do the right thing. How many times had he told her of his love for Noelle?

"He won't care," Minnie said quietly. "The only thing he listens to is his profit and his desire for prestige. My mother will be pleased to hear I've been treated well, and perhaps she would be willing to lend her voice to your cause, but he often ignores her just as much."

The expression on Hugh's face was just as hopeless as she felt. In the end, Margaret would marry Lord Milliken, and Noelle would survive, or not. And there was nothing Hugh or Margaret could do about it.

HUGH SEARCHED Margaret's expression for any sign that she'd been less than honest with him. The trouble was, he didn't know her well enough to know if she'd been lying or not. Especially considering that she'd started her time here with lies. And yet, even then, Hugh could tell something was wrong with her story. Now... he couldn't rightly say. There was nothing in her speech or manner to make him think that she wasn't telling the truth.

Hadn't he already been dismayed at Arthur's calculating response to his daughter being found? So, what was the right thing to do?

He led her into Cobb's Penn, which appeared to be under construction. It was nice to see the proprietors already making improvements. One more reason for Noelle to shine for the railroad.

"I didn't get a chance to show you the delights of Noelle the first day. We have a great deal of goods people from far and wide come to purchase. A railroad would make it easier to supply, increasing the town's size and stature."

"It would do so for any town the railroad came to," Margaret said absently, looking around the store. Avis, one of the brides who'd come to Noelle, came out from behind the counter to greet her.

"Hello, Minnie. Is there anything I can help you find today?"

The warm smiles the women exchanged made Hugh feel guilty for so quickly deciding Margaret had to go home. She'd clearly made friends here.

"No. Hugh was just showing me around. I'm glad to see where you'll be working, and I look forward to visiting you again in the future to see all the changes you're making. I'll let you get back to work."

Why did Margaret have to be so... good-hearted? It would have been easier to send someone like Maybelle home.

Margaret turned to Hugh. "One of the women I came with, Birdie, has her dressmaking business in the freight office. I was hoping to say hello to her after she was so kind to me on the journey here. The cloak I had given Minnie and then had to wear myself was poor in quality, and Birdie shared some of her fabric with me to keep me warm."

She gave Hugh a smile. "I am most grateful for her friendship, and if the railroad representatives meet people like her, they will see a place where their investment will thrive."

The confidence in her voice made him smile. Margaret was truly a kind woman and had circumstances been different, he would have enjoyed a marriage with her, getting to know her, and perhaps, even falling in love.

They said their goodbyes at the dry goods store, and continued to the freight office to say hello to Margaret's friend. It was hard, thinking of her as Margaret, particularly when she had asked to remain Minnie, but Hugh needed to keep his distance.

Jack came out, limping as he always did. "Good day to you, Hugh." Then he paused. "Or should I say, Lord Hugh? There's been talk that we've gotten it wrong all this time."

"Not at all," Hugh said, trying to remain calm. "In America, titles mean nothing, and even in England, mine is mere courtesy. I'm a man, the same as anyone else, so please continue addressing me as you always have."

He'd feared people learning of his title for this very reason. Being a man on equal level with others had given him a freedom unlike any he'd ever known. Why had Arabella arrived to ruin it all?

Even though it had come at great expense, Hugh had sent cables across the Atlantic in hopes of finding out. Surely, she didn't think they'd get married, his nephews and brother would die, and she would once again be a duke's wife? Even a duke's widow had status, so it wasn't as though she'd lost everything.

"Glad to hear it. Is there anything I can help you with?" Jack's broad grin reassured Hugh.

"I'm just showing Margaret around. I believe she was eager to say hello to Birdie."

Birdie emerged from the back, carrying several bolts of cloth. "I'm here. It's so nice of you to stop by."

Jack's grandfather, Gus, had come in, carrying more of Birdie's cloth, looking more chipper than Hugh had seen him in a long time. Even though Hugh's bride situation didn't seem to be working out, the other brides had brought a great deal of cheer to Noelle.

As Margaret and Birdie chatted amiably, Hugh once again couldn't help thinking that it was a shame she would be leaving.

Even though they'd gotten off to a rough start, he wondered if some of her original prickliness was due to her fear of discovery. Now that she was fully out in the open as Margaret, she was quite charming and friendly. And, as much as he hated to admit it, the more time he spent with her, the prettier he found her.

If there was a way to defy Margaret's father without putting the town in jeopardy, Hugh would do it. But if Arthur was willing to marry off his daughter to one of England's most profligate scoundrels to make her a countess, he couldn't see the man accepting her marriage to the assayer of a small mining town.

Hugh might be a duke's son, but it meant nothing when Margaret would never get a title of her own, nor would their children. He looked over at her, noticing how she chattered with Birdie over a piece of fabric. Margaret would be happier without a title. If only that mattered to her father.

When they were finished, Hugh showed her around the rest of the town. There hadn't been much to see, but he hoped it gave Margaret a favorable impression.

As for Hugh, he needed a break from the woman. Now, she annoyed him in a different way. She was too nice, too kind, too beautiful, and when she looked at him with those clear blue eyes of hers, he thought she was silently reminding him of the terrible fate she faced. He returned her to *La Maison*, grateful that one of the ladies said Arabella had retreated to her room, pleading a headache. At least Margaret would have some peace.

A trip to the telegraph office showed that some of his inquiries had been answered. Lord Milliken was every bit as awful as Margaret had made him out to be. In some ways, worse. Several brothels had shown him the curb because of the violent way he'd treated the women, and he'd already accrued a large gambling debt in anticipation of his marriage.

Was this the fate Hugh wanted for her?

Could he live with himself, delivering her to her father's men?

But could he also live with himself, knowing that his desire to save Margaret just might be the town's downfall? What would Arthur Coveney do if they didn't hand Margaret over?

He'd gotten nothing back about Arabella, though he hadn't expected an answer so soon. The more he dwelled upon his brother's death, the more he had to wonder if she would have been so cold as to have had a hand in it. His brother had been an excellent hunter, and her vague answer of a hunting accident seemed improbable.

Even though he'd sent a cable home, he decided to send another message. His man of business had gone on to other things, but they still sometimes corresponded. Perhaps, for old times' sake, and a shared hatred of Arabella, his friend would dig deeper into John's death.

Now that business had been taken care of, Hugh wandered back to his office. He wasn't expecting ore, but it would be nice to be surprised. But maybe their hope wasn't in gold. The mountains held other valuable minerals. What if their ore had other things that could put, and keep, Noelle on the map.

Maybe then, they wouldn't need Margaret's father's

approval because what they had was more valuable than the coal the man provided.

Definitely a dream that was more fantasy than fact, but it could happen. Chase had asked him to find an alternative bride, and as Hugh looked around the town, there didn't seem to be any other options.

CHAPTER 5

THE FOURTH DAY OF CHRISTMAS

DECEMBER 28, 1876

The day before had been pleasant for Minnie, seeing the town, and getting to know the people in Noelle better. However, it only deepened her disappointment that Hugh was no longer willing to marry her. What was the point in this charade when she would be returning home?

Yesterday was another wedding that wasn't hers, and she was surprised at how much it had affected her. As terrified as she'd been of her wedding night, she wished she'd been brave enough to endure it that first night.

She went down to the parlor as she always did in the mornings, and was starting to feel sad at the diminishing number of ladies. She might not have established deep friendships with any of them yet, but their company was a welcome respite from Arabella's nastiness.

Madame Bonheur was standing in the center of the

parlor, taking stock. She turned to glare at Minnie. "I hope you people are happy, ruining my business. I'm sure the Reverend is quite pleased with himself, the mess he's making of things. Mark my words, you will all pay."

Even though Minnie did not approve of the woman's business, it must be difficult to have her life uprooted like that. At least Minnie could ease her frustration.

"I'm sure everything will be all right," she said pleasantly in French.

The other woman looked at her blankly, like she had no idea what Minnie was saying. Minnie knew her French was just fine. She and Birdie, who was from Quebec, had spent yesterday speaking French. But the way Madame looked at her, Minnie knew she didn't understand a word. Madame, too, wasn't who she said she was.

Maybe that was the beauty of life in Noelle. You might have been born one way, but that didn't mean you had to stay that way. Who else in this town had taken on a new identity for whatever reason? Maybe this was a place to become who you wanted to be. When she'd first gotten here, she'd been playacting at being Minnie. But here, now, with Margaret's future on the line, she truly could be the woman she dreamed of being.

She gave Madame a smile. "I am truly sorry for any inconvenience we have caused."

Minnie walked into the kitchen, where breakfast was being prepared. She hadn't done much more in the past than make tea, but as she remembered the complicated stove in Hugh's kitchen, and how he'd told her that she would learn, she realized the cooking was a skill she would need regardless. If Hugh didn't want to marry her, fine. Minnie would find another way to freedom, and she would still need the skills to survive on her own.

"Is there something I can help you with?" she asked Milly, the cook, who was stirring something on the stove.

Milly turned to her. "What are you doing, messing in my kitchen?"

Minnie smiled at her. "I'm not trying to intrude. Nor do I want to take your place. When I'm married, I will need to operate my husband's stove. I don't know how to cook. If I learned, it would help me survive better here in Noelle."

At first, Minnie was sure the cook was going to say no. But then she nodded slowly. "I hear you're a real lady," she said.

She would have to answer this question for a while. Maybe that's why so many people hid who they all were. Why Hugh had never told anyone he was a lord. Even now, she noticed how people seemed more in awe of him, and gave him a little more deference than they used to. He obviously hadn't wanted to capitalize on his title, but wanted to live a new life. She couldn't understand why anyone wouldn't want to be a lord, but maybe being one wasn't everything it was cut out to be. After all, the one she was supposed to marry was certainly no prize.

"I'm just the same as anyone else here," Minnie said. "I'm here to start a new life, and my days of being a wealthy, pampered girl are over."

Milly looked doubtful. Minnie squared her shoulders. "Aren't there things in your past you'd prefer other people not know, or maybe that you've learned and grown from, and are choosing to live differently? I don't want to be the woman I was in Denver. I want to be part of this place, contributing the best I can."

A look of understanding crossed Milly's face. But then she shook her head. "I hear people are coming to take you home."

Minnie nodded slowly. "I'm hoping to convince them

otherwise. But even if I go home with them now, I will be back."

It was a bold statement, considering she had no idea how that would ever happen. Not with the way her parents guarded her every move. They'd certainly be even more on guard when she returned. But she couldn't go back to that life. Even if her family agreed that she wasn't going to marry Lord Milliken, they would still want her to marry someone else of their choosing. And they had entirely different ideas about her happiness.

Whatever Minnie had said, it had convinced Milly. Because she gestured to the stove, and before Minnie knew it, she was wearing an apron, learning how to cook.

WHEN HUGH ARRIVED at *La Maison*, he was surprised to find Margaret in the kitchen, helping prepare breakfast.

"I thought you couldn't cook," he said.

Margaret gave him a dazzling smile that made something deep in his heart ache. "It was time I learned. Milly has been good enough to give me some lessons. If you're hungry, you should sit and have some breakfast. You can test my new skill."

He didn't move. Instead, he stared at her. "It's nice you want to find a way to pass the time, but you'll be going home soon, and it seems that is a waste of both your time and Milly's."

Margaret glared at him. "How can you say that? Learning new skills is not a waste of time. I will never again be the helpless girl I was. Besides, I don't want to go back. I want to stay in Noelle. You spent the past few days showing me what a wonderful place it is, sharing the town's vision. How can I go back?"

This was not the result he'd had in mind. Especially because Margaret seemed so out of place here. But as he looked at her earnestly shining eyes, he realized that while she had a lot to learn, he never once thought she didn't fit in. How many people had looked at him as a lord, and thought he belonged in a ballroom instead of playing with metal? He hadn't found such freedom until coming here. Maybe they weren't so different after all.

But just as Hugh felt his heart softening towards her, he shook his head. The difference between them was that he was free to stay here. He had no obligations, whatever Arabella claimed, to return home. Margaret, on the other hand, did.

"And what of the family who misses you?" he asked.

Margaret shook her head sadly. "My family misses me just as much as Arabella misses her sons. They see me as a tool, not a person they care about. I am their showpiece, and my accomplishments serve to highlight how wonderful they are, but they have not once considered what makes me happy."

She looked thoughtful for a moment, like she wasn't sure she wanted to continue, but then she straightened and looked him directly in the eye. "No one asked me if I wanted to marry Lord Milliken. They told me. He didn't even have the courtesy to propose. A girl spends her whole life dreaming of the moment a man will propose to her, but instead, I got something very different. He took me on a drive and told me that since we were to be married, we should be seen together."

Margaret frowned. And her frown turned to something that looked almost like dejection. She looked up at him. "You have done the best job of courting me of anyone. You wanted me to be comfortable, and you treated me with respect. You might not have spoken of love, but you have to understand, that was a luxury I've never been allowed."

She dished some food out onto a plate, then set it on the table. "Eat before it gets cold."

Then she dished out plates for the women who'd begun trickling into the room. She brought her own to the table, sat and dug into her meal. At the first bite, she looked incredibly pleased.

"This isn't terrible," she said. "I made this myself, and it's good."

Milly banged the spoon on the pot. "Of course, it's good. I taught you."

"It's delicious," Mrs. Walters said. "You're a fast learner."

The other ladies murmured in agreement. Why did they all have to be so encouraging to Margaret? They weren't making his job any easier.

Margaret smiled and took another bite. Then she looked up at Hugh. "You should at least try it. It would be rude not to."

He couldn't help smiling at her words. Deep down, she couldn't hide her breeding. But along with that breeding, there was an inherent kindness and gentleness to her that many women in his class did not possess. It was one of the reasons he had avoided the marriage market in England. So many vain and shallow women like Arabella, all pretty little dolls with their so-called accomplishments, but not a drop of substance.

What a cruel trick that the woman sitting before him had both.

Hugh took a seat. Margaret was quietly eating her breakfast, but her eyes were upon him. What if the food was terrible? Would he be able to tell her the truth without hurting her feelings? But when he took a bite, it was indeed quite good. She wouldn't be preparing gourmet meals, but she could make eggs, and people could survive on eggs. A man could survive quite a long time on them, actually.

"What's that smile about?" Margaret asked.

"I was thinking that eggs were the first dish I learned how to make. They're simple but filling. It's a good skill to have. I'm glad you're learning, but I fear you will have little use for it when you go home."

She set her fork down with a *thud*. "Why are you so insistent on sending me home? Do I displease you so much that you cannot stand the sight of me? I know my deception was wrong, but you, too, were less than honest about your origins. And I'm finding, the more I notice about others in this town, they also have their secrets. Perhaps it was wrong of me to lie about my identity, but we all have things we want to hide."

What on earth was she talking about? And then he thought about his friends and the gaps in their stories, or the pieces of the past that only came out after too much drink. But it wasn't the same.

"Yes, but you are a young lady of means. You have a family who loves you."

He stopped at his words. Hadn't Margaret already told him she was merely property to her family? That all her family wanted for her was an advantageous match which would make them look good? All she wanted for herself was the very thing he had come to Noelle in search of. Why was he more worthy of that life than she? Suddenly, he felt like a heel. Unfortunately, there were greater reasons for getting Margaret to cooperate than just her background.

"I'm sorry, Margaret, you're right. I know you want a new life for yourself, but the difference is, in running away, you're defying a powerful man. Have you not thought of the consequences of angering your father? What do you think he will do to the people who help you thwart his plans?"

Her face turned white. She looked almost like she was going to be sick. "I saw him beat a stable boy once for stealing from the kitchen," she said quietly. "It was just an apple, and I hadn't eaten mine that day. It cost us nothing, but he was so irate at being stolen from."

Tears ran down her face. "I'm his property just as much as that apple. I don't want to be Margaret anymore. I'd hoped that by remaining Minnie, I could have a new life."

Then she took her handkerchief and dabbed at her eyes, becoming once more the lady of the manor. "I shall make it clear to my father that no one in this town did anything wrong. That's why you've been showing me around, isn't it? You want to keep me happy. Yes, you wanted me to speak well of Noelle to my father, but more than that, you wanted it known that I was in no way mistreated. You can rest assured, my father will hear no complaints from me."

She returned to eating her breakfast, only now it looked more like a chore and that the joy it had just given her was gone. She ate slowly, methodically, and properly.

It had only taken a few words to kill the spirit he'd seen bubbling inside her. For a moment, he almost felt guilty for being the cause. But Margaret had to accept reality. She was right. She was as much her father's property as the apple the stable boy had stolen.

Margaret had told him that she was willing to learn, and here she was, learning. Though he suspected that many of the other brides also lacked skills in the kitchen, she was the only one he'd seen approach the cook and ask for lessons. Or maybe she was the only one Milly had given lessons to. He honestly didn't know, but seeing Margaret make the effort did something funny in his heart. He already was questioning sending her home, and now, those questions weighed even more loudly in his head. Even though she didn't know all the things she needed to for life in Noelle, he saw in her a willing partner. Which to him was worth more than all the skill in the world. But how is he supposed to reconcile the fact that her father wanted her back? More importantly, she had a fiancé waiting for her. A man she'd promised to marry.

He looked up at her. "Tell me about your fiancé. If you don't want to go back to him, why did you agree to marry him?"

Margaret set her fork down and folded her hands in her lap. "You ask as though I had a choice. I can assure you I did not. As with everything in my life, I was told whom I would marry. I was never given the opportunity to court like a normal person. I've only been allowed to associate with the people my parents think are appropriate. The only person I could ever truly count on as a friend was Minnie. I suppose it's odd to be close to one's maid, and in front of my family, I had to hide my true affection for her. But she was always the only person with whom I could be myself. The so-called friends my parents put in my life were people who only thought to gain an advantage by our acquaintance. Were I to share any secrets with them, they were likely to use them against me."

Hadn't that been his life? People bowing to him and flattering him in hopes he would put in a good word for them with the duke. He might have been the third son, but with such a powerful father, everyone wanted an association with Hugh. Even Arabella, whom he thought truly loved him for himself, had only been after his connections. She wasn't here out of love for him, but out of a desire to use him once more.

"I'm sorry," Hugh said. "I understand better than you think. In England, all anyone cared about was my title, most particularly access to my father's. I want to help you, but surely you know what angering a man like your father could mean for me, but most particularly, for this town."

A sad look crossed Margaret's face, and for a moment, he

thought she might cry. "All he wants is for me to have an advantageous marriage. I don't think he cares who it is. Anything to elevate himself."

She looked at him with hope and longing, and he knew that she was hoping that his rank could be used to help her.

"I have no title, only the courtesy title of the son of the duke. In England, I am called Lord Hugh, but that means nothing."

Margaret nodded slowly. "I'm afraid I don't know much about any of that. When my parents met Lord Milliken, that's all they looked at. I'm sure my father's men investigated whatever they investigate about a person, but sometimes I wonder if they looked beyond his title. I've been told that my intended is not a very good person."

Hugh already knew Margaret's fiancé was a profligate son who had spent the family fortune on gambling and women and now needed a wealthy bride to fill the family coffers. He had no respect for such men, preying on women to cover their own faults. If a man were to lose the family fortune, he should find an honorable way of restoring it. True, people back home didn't see marrying for wealth as being dishonorable, but that was one more area in which he disagreed with the other members of his class.

But none of this would help her. His only hope was that he could discover something truly foul about her fiancé that would make her father cry off. He looked at Margaret. "I don't wish to give you false hope, but I have sent out some inquiries about your intended. Perhaps I will uncover something your father hasn't, and he will call off the wedding. Otherwise, there's nothing I can do."

Milly stomped over with a pot of coffee. "Coffee?"

He nodded. "Thank you."

She started pouring it into his cup, but quickly turned

and dumped it on him. Hugh jumped, giving a shout. "What did you do that for?"

"How could you dash her dreams like that? All she wants is the same as any of us. And what makes us so much better than her that she can't have it? You terrible, selfish man. I thought you were one of the good ones, but you're not. You're sending her away without a fight. Have you even asked her father if she might stay?"

Then she turned to Margaret. "I know telegrams are expensive, but you should send a message to your father and ask him if there's any way you might stay."

Margaret nodded. Then she picked up her now-empty plate along with Hugh's soggy breakfast and stood. "I believe I will, thank you. I don't have much money, but it should be enough. It's too bad those chickens or that goose aren't here so I can feed them these scraps."

As she turned toward the door, Mrs. Walters touched her arm. "If you don't have enough money, I can give you some. I'll also do what I can to help you find a way to stay."

"Thank you," Margaret murmured, sounding so grateful that Hugh felt even more like a heel.

"No one should be forced into a marriage with a monster," Mrs. Walters said, glaring at him.

Margaret went to the back door, leaving Hugh to face the wrath of the women in the kitchen. He'd underestimated just how much they'd come to care for her. But how could he not, when he felt the same way?

"Now get out of my kitchen," Milly said. "The likes of you aren't welcome here."

He looked back at her. "But in the past, you said-"

"That was then, this is now. I liked you because you always seemed to take a person at face value, and you treated everyone as an equal. But that dear girl is terrified of going home, and I cannot understand why you would make her the sacrificial lamb."

What other choice did they have? He couldn't see Arthur Coveney being convinced to let his daughter stay in this town without good reason. But what reason could they give? There was nothing to interest the man. If the railroad didn't come here, it would go to another town. Though he and the others thought Noelle was special, he wasn't sure how to convince a man only interested in the bottom line of that same worth.

Draven entered the room. "We need to talk," he said, looking at Hugh. "Alone."

He followed Draven outside. The concerned expression on his friend's face worried him. "What's going on?"

"Coveney's men arrived, and I don't like the looks of them."

"How bad are they?"

"Not the sort I'd feel safe sending my enemy's daughter with, let alone Coveney's. I don't know what the man was thinking, using them, but they don't look right."

Hugh didn't like the sound of it either. "Where are they now?"

"I told them Miss Coveney was being entertained by some of the town's finest, and I would fetch her. I took them across the street to the saloon, and made sure they were given strong drinks. They were quickly joined by the ladies, who are frustrated at not being able to work the way they usually do. Coveney's men seemed more than happy to be entertained by them."

"We can't keep them there forever," Hugh said. "But the more I talked to Margaret, the more I know it would be wrong to send her home."

Draven nodded. "Can we afford the trouble if we don't send her back?"

For a few moments, neither man said anything. There was nothing to say. Not with so much at risk.

"We still need another bride," Draven said. "We're already a bride short, and Chase is nervous that there aren't enough women to go around. Have you taken another look at Madame's girls to see if we could make that work?"

"We'll figure something out," Hugh said. "There's still time. I know Chase is nervous, but we can make it work. We'll find a way."

Draven looked at him a little too knowingly. "You still want her for yourself."

He didn't want to admit it, not to Draven, not even to himself. Not when it looked so hopeless.

"We can't let them take her," Hugh said.

"I'll send a message to Coveney, making sure the men are on the up and up. A wealthy heiress like that, it wouldn't be unheard of for outlaws to have seen the signs about her and come to take the prize for themselves."

"At least if we buy some time, we can figure out a new solution for Minnie," Hugh said.

Draven stared at him for a moment. "It might be easier for you if you call her Margaret instead of Minnie. The more you distance yourself from her, the easier it will be to let her go."

The name had slipped out. He'd been trying to do so for the same reason Draven had just stated. But the more Hugh thought about her, the more it seemed wrong not to call her Minnie.

"She wants nothing to do with Margaret. She wants to be Minnie. She likes the freedom of having a new name. And I don't blame her. One of the happiest days of my life was when I dropped the 'lord' and became just Hugh."

Draven shook his head. "Coveney could charge us with kidnapping. Could charge you with kidnapping."

He wouldn't do anyone any good from jail, and even though he knew his friend was sympathetic, there wasn't anything he could do.

"Let's keep the men busy and get confirmation from Coveney that these are his men. It wouldn't hurt to keep an eye on them, either. If they're as rough as you say, perhaps we can find a reason to put them in jail."

Draven grinned. "Maybe you're not willing to admit it yet, but we'll be attending your wedding before long. I just hope you're smart about it. You could ruin us all."

Did he love Minnie? Hugh couldn't say for sure. But he knew that no woman deserved that kind of life. No man, either, for that matter.

"Do what you can to keep the men busy, and I'll keep Minnie out of sight. No sense in forcing something before it's time."

Draven nodded then turned to walk away. Hugh went back inside, where Margaret was waiting expectantly. "The men are here, aren't they?"

Hugh nodded. "But we're not sure they're the right ones. What sort of men work for your father?"

She shrugged. "I don't know. He doesn't bring his business home much. There are his guards, of course, and they often follow us. But we aren't allowed to speak."

Instead of being comforted by her words, he was concerned. Coveney wasn't going to let his daughter go easily.

"We're doing our best to keep you safe," he told her. "But I'll need your help. I need you to stay out of sight and out of the way. If the men see you, they might snatch you, and we cannot protect you."

She nodded. "So, you are trying to help me."

"As much as I can. But if your father confirms that these are his men, there's nothing I can do."

She looked pained by his answer. He hated that he couldn't give her a better one.

"I understand," she said. "Perhaps I can go visit Birdie. We enjoy each other's company, and it will keep me from worrying."

At least she had friends who could temporarily hide her. It wouldn't be much protection, but at least they could keep moving her around to protect her for a while.

"You'll have to stay in the background. You can't be seen in public. Right now, the men are busy in the saloon. But who knows how long that will last, and when they'll decide to go looking for you."

She nodded thoughtfully. "I can't stay here," she said. "They also know that this is where I'm staying. And I'm sure Arabella would be all too happy to tell them exactly where I sleep at night."

He hadn't thought about that. Unfortunately, she was right. Arabella would do anything to get rid of competition.

Milly looked at them sympathetically. "It's not much, but Minnie could stay in my room. At least if the men come for her, and Arabella tries to give her away, they won't be able to find her. Unless they search the house, but I have a few hiding spots. Madame has had me hide many a husband from a jealous wife."

"Thank you," Minnie said. "Let me get my things and we can be off."

As she left the room, Hugh tried not to think about all the things that could go wrong. But as long as Minnie stayed hidden, he could look into Coveney's supposed men. If they weren't on the up and up, perhaps it would be just what they needed to convince Coveney to let his daughter stay.

CHAPTER 6

THE FIFTH DAY OF CHRISTMAS

DECEMBER 29, 1876

Her father's men had continued to be occupied at the saloon, giving Minnie more time to convince Hugh to let her stay. To further thwart the men until they received confirmation that they did belong to her father, Hugh had suggested they go on a sleigh ride.

"Are you comfortable?" he asked, tucking a blanket closer around her.

"Yes, thank you."

His attention to her comfort made her smile. The longer she stayed in Noelle, the more she felt like Minnie. And, given that everyone seemed to respect her wishes to be called Minnie, it made it easier to become the new persona. As she sat, huddled next to him, surrounded by plenty of warm blankets, she could almost pretend that this was a pleasant outing. This must be what courting was like, except, of course, they weren't. Still, as she sat so close to Hugh, she liked the feeling of having him near. He smelled good, of soap and warmth, and something else she couldn't quite place, except that she found it intriguing.

Lord Milliken always smelled too much of alcohol and cheap perfume. When she commented it on it to her mother, her mother told her that a lady ignores such things. But how terrible to spend one's life pretending one couldn't smell her husband's foul stench. She would much rather spend her life breathing in the warm scent of Hugh.

He looked down at her and smiled. "Are you warm enough?"

"Perfectly," she said, smiling back at him. "It's nice, being here with you. I find this ever so much more pleasant than riding in my father's carriage. There are bricks for warmth, but I find having you close to me keeps me warmer."

He stiffened. "You know this isn't appropriate, right? Your fiancé and your father might consider this taking too many liberties."

She let out a long sigh. "Technically, I'm ruined already, having run off the way I did. True, the beginning of my journey was with women, but I've been alone with you many times unchaperoned. Even if we weren't sitting so close, Society would view our time together as inappropriate. So why not enjoy ourselves?"

"Don't go falling in love with me. No good will come of it. Guard your heart, because otherwise the rest of your life will be miserable, married to another."

His words made her feel like a child. Like her mother was speaking to her. She'd cautioned Margaret against falling in love, telling her that love only made fools of people. But sitting here, next to Hugh, in a mostly companionable way, she couldn't imagine a life without it.

"You still think I'm going to marry him, don't you?"

"You have no choice. If an agreement has been made, whether or not you are party to it is immaterial under the law. You know that."

"And what if he cries off? Perhaps he will see my time here as a blemish on my character."

He shook his head. "If his sole inducement in marrying you is your money, it will matter not."

Once again, his words gave her little encouragement. Of course, Milliken's only reason for marrying her was money. They'd hardly spent any time in one another's company.

She turned and looked at him. "Tell me this. If you had a sister and she was marrying a horrible man, what would you do to stop it?"

"My family is wealthy enough and important enough that if I had a sister, she would not need to make such a marriage. I am sure we would make sure he was an honorable man."

Why did he have to be so difficult?

"And if you discover that the man you thought was an honorable man was, in fact, dishonorable?"

He looked thoughtful for a moment. "You think that your intended's objectionable qualities are not known to your father?"

She would like to think that. But surely, he must know about some of the man's misbehaviors.

Though Minnie knew in her heart that her father probably didn't care about Milliken's misdeeds, it felt good to know Hugh at least was willing to hear her out. Once again, she regretted not marrying him when she'd first arrived. So many of their problems would have been solved if only she wasn't so terrified of what the wedding night entailed. As she looked at Hugh again, she couldn't imagine him humiliating her. Even though she had been told that the experience was always uncomfortable and unpleasant for a woman, she would like to think that a man such as he would do his best to make it as comfortable and pleasant as he could.

"I like it here and I want to stay," Minnie said, hoping to turn the conversation to more pleasant things. "This is exactly what I hoped for, what we'd hoped for, when we thought of sending Minnie here."

"You don't find it uncivilized?"

Minnie shook her head. "On the contrary. I find it more civilized than most of Society. In Society, we all say and do the right things, even if we don't mean them. We are kind to one another's faces. But then as soon as one's back is turned, the claws come out."

He murmured sympathetically. Of course, he would understand. Hadn't he rejected the same Society? They had so much in common, if only she could convince him to fight for her.

A gust of wind hit, and she snuggled closer to Hugh. So very improper and un-Margaret-like, and it felt wonderful. And even though Hugh had just lectured her on propriety, he pulled her closer to him. "It does get cold up here. I know you want to stay, but keep in mind that this time of year, you'll be cold like this often."

"It wasn't cold in your shop. "

"True. But come summer, you'll find the heat almost unbearable. "

"I thought that's what the windows were for," she said, smiling at him. She'd been paying attention, and hopefully he saw that. Could he see she was willing to make an effort and do the right thing?

Hugh didn't answer, which she took as a sign that he was noticing all the reasons Minnie had to stay. Could she get him to see reason?

"You mentioned that you'd like to build a house for your family someday," she said, "Have you thought about where?"

He let out a long, satisfied sigh. Clearly, he had, and she appreciated that about him.

"I always thought it would be something I decided upon with my wife. However, when you're entering Noelle, if you turn left toward the hills instead of right into town, there's a small bluff, which overlooks the town and the river and I like to go there to think sometimes. I own the land, and I hope my future wife would be in agreement about building there. But if not, we'll find something we can agree upon. Still, it is the nicest piece of property I've ever seen."

It hurt that Hugh spoke of his future wife, and not of her. She hated that he was still unwilling to consider marrying her when she was trying to think of every way possible to make it so.

"How far is it from here? I would love to see this place if you're willing to take me there," Minnie said, smiling at him.

For a moment, Hugh looked like he was going to refuse. Obviously, he didn't want her getting any ideas about that being the place for her future home.

"I suppose, if we take the long way around, we can get there without being noticed by the saloon's occupants. As I said, it's just land, and the person would have to have quite an imagination in order to see the potential that I see."

Minnie could imagine many things, and if it meant spending more time with Hugh and letting him picture her as part of his vision, she could make her imaginings even stronger.

The snow was deep in spots, and the sled slid right over it. In others, Hugh had to be creative to go around the areas that were already turning to dry ground.

"It's so beautiful here, I want to share it with everyone." Then Minnie looked up at him. "However, if Noelle were to become too crowded, I think it would lose its charm. I hope, when the railroad comes in the mayor's vision comes to pass, it's doesn't become too spoiled with people."

"I agree. And I don't think Charlie will allow that to happen. We all want Noelle to be successful, but I think we all hope to keep our town this sweet little piece of heaven."

As they neared the top of a small hill, Minnie looked down upon the town. The buildings were small and sparse, yet they held the promise of something wonderful to come.

Then Hugh stopped the sleigh. "This is it," he said. "In the summer, I sometimes sleep out here, imagining what it would be like. You wouldn't believe the number of stars you can see at night. It's a peaceful place, and as the town grows, it will still be close enough for entertainment, but not so close you feel that everyone is on top of you."

As Minnie followed his gaze, she could see why he loved it so much. And she, too, could see the advantage of being so close yet so far. It wasn't like being isolated out on a ranch as one of the new brides was. But she would still have her privacy.

"If the railroad comes, where will it go?"

Hugh pointed at a place near the river. "There. The railroad will mostly follow the river, as it is easier for trains to take on water as they need, and the ground is already cut out. The railroad does not have to do as much blasting or use as much labor when there is already a natural path."

She liked how he explained things to her and didn't talk to her as though she were stupid. Often times, men didn't take the opportunity to let a woman in their plans. But Hugh seemed to respect her, and once again, Minnie thought that she couldn't have found a better man to be a husband.

Another blast of icy air hit, making Minnie shiver. Hugh wrapped his arms around her. "I thought I'd prepared enough for the cold, but perhaps I was wrong. It's chillier than I had expected. I'm sorry."

The cold didn't matter if it meant Minnie could stay in Hugh's arms. More and more, she found that there was no other place she would rather be. Perhaps this was the secret of what made women decide to fall from grace. Her mother had never told her about the tingly feeling she Minnie inside when Hugh touched her. She couldn't imagine experiencing this with anyone else. Why must Hugh be so stubborn?

She looked up at him and smiled. "I don't mind. I'm glad you brought me here, and I shall cherish this time always."

He met her gaze, but then he shook his head. "We can't do this. You are promised to another, and your father could quite literally kill me for taking advantage of you."

"How are you taking advantage of me? I'm here because I want to be. We've done nothing wrong."

Something changed in his expression, and for a moment, Minnie was almost frightened. But then the tingly feeling inside her grew, and she felt… excited.

"But I want to," he murmured, looking away.

Was this what people whispered about, but no one would discuss with Margaret? Whatever wrong Hugh feared committing, something inside her wanted it just as much.

He adjusted the reins, like he was going to leave, but Minnie placed her hand on his arm. "Please. Let us stay here a while longer. I want…"

He looked down upon her, and she could see the hunger in his eyes. Over the past several days, she'd seen some of the other couples embracing, and it had created a longing inside her. There had to be a difference between the humiliation her mother had described, and whatever was happening between the new brides and their grooms. But how was Minnie to know, if he still refused to marry her?

"Don't say it. I'm doing everything I can as a gentleman to do the right thing. Right now, you're asking too much of me."

Returning his attention to the horses, he made a noise,

then gave the reins a quick jerk. The sleigh took off in a burst of speed, and they practically flew down the hill. It was exhilarating, and it almost erased the emptiness of being rejected. Though she knew little about the ways of men and women, she knew Hugh felt something for her.

While she could agree in principle that defying her father could be dangerous, how was she supposed to return to such an unbearable life when she'd had a taste of freedom? How could she marry a man who made her skin crawl when she'd been so close to marrying one who made everything inside her come alive?

THE WOMAN WAS GOING to drive him mad. Hugh gripped the reins tightly as they returned to town. He was supposed to keep her out longer, but he was at great risk of kissing her senseless if they remained alone together. And then he'd face Coveney's wrath for sure. In England, it would be swords or pistols at dawn. But here, a man shot first and asked questions later.

Stealing a glance at Minnie, he knew that he'd hurt her feelings. Given what he knew of her background, the idea of romance was entirely foreign to her. She was falling in love for the first time, and he was refusing to give way to those feelings.

He briefly closed his eyes. Falling in love. Was that really what was happening between them? True, his feelings for Minnie were deeper than he'd ever experienced with anyone else. With Arabella, he'd been a giddy boy, making a fool of himself. But what he felt had lacked maturity and wisdom. Now, he knew better. And he knew that loving someone also meant behaving with honor. Perhaps he did love Minnie, but she was not his to love, and whatever emotion he had growing inside him was best put aside.

As for whatever Minnie was going through, he could chalk it up to being a milestone on the path to adulthood. But he hated the idea that he may very well be the one to break her heart. Why couldn't she understand that he had no choice?

None of his contacts had given him any useful information that he could go to Arthur Coveney with. And Coveney still had not answered any of the telegrams sent him after his initial response that he was sending someone for Margaret.

So, what was a man to do?

Hugh stole a glance at Minnie, who'd turned away from him. From the way she held herself, he could tell she was deeply wounded. Better for her heart to break now, before they were too attached. Who was he kidding? He was already too attached. The pain he'd felt at Arabella's betrayal had so quickly dissipated that he hardly remembered it now.

It would take a lifetime to recover from losing Minnie, if such a thing were even possible.

As much he hated to admit it, whatever was happening between them wasn't as easily explained away as a passing fancy.

Such a cruel trick, to be so close to love, but for it to seem so far away. He couldn't just give her up, yet he had no idea how to convince her father that the lord she needed was not the one they intended for her.

CHAPTER 7

THE SIXTH DAY OF CHRISTMAS

DECEMBER 30, 1876

Hugh counted it a blessing that they'd managed to go another day without Coveney's supposed men finding Minnie. He'd stopped by the saloon to find they were still occupied. If only Coveney would respond to the telegrams he'd sent. Surely the man would want to know his daughter wasn't falling into the hands of bandits.

But what if Minnie's father didn't care? What if he just wanted the prestige of having a lord for a son-in-law?

As much as he didn't want to spend any more time getting attached to Minnie, he couldn't bring himself to stay away from her.

While Hugh had been escorting Minnie the previous day, Draven had declared his love for, then married, Pearl, the woman who was only supposed to be pretending to be a bride. Maybe Draven's advice about love hadn't been so much about Hugh's conundrum, but about Draven's romantic struggles. Though Hugh was genuinely happy for his friend, he couldn't help being jealous of all the marriages happening around him.

The whole point in bringing mail-order brides to Noelle was for the men to get married. Only Hugh's bride was so out of reach, he didn't know how he was ever going to get her down the aisle.

He went around to the back of *La Maison*, hoping to both avoid Arabella, and to see Minnie.

Why did he torture himself like this?

Milly stood guard at the back door. "What do you want?"

"To see Minnie."

She looked at him like she wanted to gut him like a trout or some other creature she planned on serving for dinner.

"She's busy."

There wasn't much she could possibly be doing, not with trying to stay out of sight of everyone.

But Milly didn't seem like she cared to argue that point. Or any point for that matter. Mostly, she just looked like she wanted Hugh gone.

"Let him in," Minnie said. He couldn't see her, but at least she confirmed that she was within.

Milly stepped aside, and when Hugh entered the kitchen, he saw Minnie rolling out some kind of dough.

"I'm learning how to make bread," she said, smiling.

It was wrong of him to think about how beautiful she looked with splotches of flour on her face. But he couldn't help himself. At least he had enough self-control not to reach out and kiss her.

"I hope you'll let me taste it when it's finished. My breakfast the other day was ruined." He sent a pointed glance to Milly, who shrugged.

Even though it was frustrating to have such a strict guard

over Minnie, it was comforting to know that the cook would be even more protective if Coveney's men showed up. He'd heard stories about her abilities with a gun, which gave him even more comfort.

Minnie was safe here.

Arabella screeched from the other room, reminding him that safety was an illusion.

"That woman," Milly muttered.

Everyone was losing patience with Arabella, it seemed, and Hugh had no idea of how to get her to leave town. He'd already rejected her in the strongest way possible, yet she still clung to the crazy idea that he'd return with her and somehow become duke.

The sound of her footsteps came closer.

Minnie sighed and put down the rolling pin. "I'll go hide in your room. Hugh, you should probably go, too. Last night, I heard her fussing about how you weren't paying any attention to her."

He'd been too busy paying attention to Minnie. When he wasn't with her, he might as well have been, for all the time he spent thinking about her.

"I have a better idea," he said. "I just went past the saloon, and your father's men are still distracted. Let's go for a walk to get some fresh air."

It was a stupid suggestion, considering yesterday's drive had been such a disaster. No, not a disaster. But it had put thoughts in both of their hearts that didn't belong there. At least if they went for a walk, they wouldn't be in such intimate quarters as they'd been in the sleigh. She couldn't snuggle close to him, and he wouldn't feel her warmth.

Minnie's face lit up, and he wanted to hate himself for how much pleasure it gave him to delight her so.

"That would be lovely. If it's safe, I'd like to say hello to my friends and see how they're doing. Maybe it sounds silly, but with as restrictive as my family has been, I've never had friends to call on like this."

He could have done without the reminder of the life he was returning her to.

More and more, he knew she belonged here in Noelle. But there was a very powerful man who needed convincing otherwise.

She put on her wrap, and he noticed that she had a new scarf she hadn't had the day before. Probably a gift from one of the other ladies. His heart twisted again at the thought of sending her away from this.

As they came to the corner of *La Maison*, he made her stop so he could make sure it was safe. He spotted a tussle at the saloon. Madame stood at the entrance, shotgun in hand, and the man was running out the door, pulling up his pants. Hugh recognized him immediately. One of Minnie's father's men.

He quickly guided Minnie in the other direction, out of sight of the saloon. Whatever the man's transgression was, it had to be bad for Madame to chase him off like that. Worse, it also meant he wouldn't be distracted from his original mission. Soon, his attention would be back on taking Minnie to her father. And if he was such a miscreant as to be forcibly removed from Madame's establishment, he wasn't the sort to be trusted with an innocent like Minnie.

He'd have to find a place for Minnie to hide, and so he could talk with Draven. Arabella Perhaps the sheriff could put the man in jail, buying them more time. Surely Coveney would want to know about the man he was trusting to bring his daughter home safely.

Arabella had entered the kitchen just as they'd exited, so *La Maison* was currently not a safe place for Minnie. Which meant he had to think of somewhere else to go.

"It looks like the men who've come to get you are no

longer occupied. We need to keep you better hidden, and you must do your part in staying out of sight."

Margaret nodded slowly. "Does this mean you're going to help me stay?"

Why did she have to continually insist on something that wasn't possible?

"I can't. But I also don't think the men who are here for you have your best interests at heart. I don't trust them, and until I am certain your father truly wants you with them, I can't hand you over."

The expression on her face told him that wasn't the answer she'd wanted. But even if he were honest with her, and told her that yes, he wanted her to stay, it would do them no good. Why get her hopes up when there was no future for them?

They entered the freight office, and Birdie immediately came out from her work area, Gus trailing behind her. "I'm so glad to see you again."

Jack also came out. "This isn't a social call, is it?"

"I'm afraid not," Hugh said. "I don't know if you heard the ruckus at the saloon, but that means the men who want to take Minnie back to Denver are going to be looking for her."

The other man nodded slowly, like he knew exactly what Hugh was referring to. "One of them stopped by earlier this morning, asking if Miss Margaret was here. Your lady friend told him that Margaret and Birdie are friends."

It wasn't proper to hurt a woman, but if Hugh could shake some sense into Arabella, he would. Because it was obvious that Arabella was putting them on Margaret's trail.

"What did you tell him?"

Jack shrugged. "That she wasn't here, and we hadn't seen her today. But he'll be back, and he made a great show of the guns on his belt."

"But we're prepared," Gus said. "We know how to handle scoundrels like them."

"I didn't mean to put you in harm's way," Minnie said quietly, looking at Birdie. "I'm so sorry. Surely they're not from my father, because while he is known for getting what he wants, I can't see him condoning this behavior."

Birdie came and put her arm around Minnie. "This isn't your fault. The men didn't have to threaten us. But now that they have, you can rest assured that we'll do everything we can to protect you. It's what friends do."

A lump filled Hugh's throat as he saw the depth of loyalty and friendship established between these two women. He wanted to do the same for Margaret, but he also couldn't risk angering her father. But maybe it was better for Margaret to have another woman standing by her rather than him.

Minnie smiled at Birdie. "That's kind of you to say, but if I hadn't run away from home, I wouldn't have put anyone here in danger. I'd only been thinking of myself, not how my leaving would impact everyone else. But if you don't mind helping me a while longer, I promise I will make it up to you."

"There is no need," Birdie said. "You were just doing what you thought was right. No one should be forced into a marriage they don't want, especially if it's with someone like the man they want you to marry. I'll help you in any way I can."

As Margaret thanked Birdie, Hugh looked at Jack. Did he feel the same way? Jack nodded slowly, as if he'd anticipated Hugh's question. "I wouldn't feel right about sending Minnie with them."

"I can trust you to keep her hidden?" Hugh asked. "I'd like to speak with Draven, and see what he has learned. But if the men come back, I need to know that Minnie will be safe."

Birdie stepped forward, looking fiercer than a sweet

woman like her should. "She'll be safe. These aren't the worst I've ever had to deal with, and I know how to keep a person hidden. Minnie is safe with us."

The emphasis on Minnie made it clear exactly what Birdie thought of his desire to keep his distance. But this wasn't the time or the place to discuss it with either woman. He gave a nod, then the tip of his hat, and went in search of the sheriff.

It seemed impossible that he could find a way to be with Minnie, but hopefully, he could at least keep her safe.

CHAPTER 8

THE SEVENTH DAY OF CHRISTMAS

DECEMBER 31, 1876

Draven had called a meeting with Hugh, Charlie, and Chase to sort out what to do about Minnie. They still hadn't heard from her father, and the men who'd come to town in search of her were getting impatient. They'd hidden Minnie in a variety of locations, but the men were getting bolder in their searches, even though Draven had made it known they were no longer welcome in Noelle and would be arrested on sight. The trouble was, Draven was one man, and he had other problems to deal with. Every time he went to take care of another situation, they'd come out of hiding long enough to cause trouble before disappearing again.

How much longer could they continue hiding Minnie without putting the town in danger?

Charlie shook his head slowly as he addressed the others. "I don't like them any more than the rest of you, but last night, when they trashed the saloon, the one called Ed said that Mr. Coveney wasn't going to be happy. I take that to mean they came from him. How are we supposed to protect her when they'll stop at nothing to get her?"

Hugh glared at him. "I didn't take you for a coward."

"It's not cowardice when you're trying to think things through so you're doing the right thing for Noelle. Draven can't find them to arrest them."

To someone who didn't know Charlie, they might think his words were full of confidence. But Hugh saw the doubt in his eyes. Deep down, Charlie was a good man, and though he wanted to protect the town at all costs, Hugh could see that he wasn't certain he was doing the right thing.

Hugh turned to Chase. "Surely you don't want her to go with them. I know you had to call Doctor Deane to attend to one of the girls who'd been roughed up by those men. Would you really entrust a young lady to their care?"

Chase shook his head. "It was Angelique. They hurt her pretty bad. I can't imagine Minnie's father would approve."

If they'd hurt a girl who was more child than woman, what would they do to Minnie? Though Chase didn't think Coveney would approve, he was the one who'd sent the men.

"Angelique is different than a man's daughter," Charlie said. "I don't want to send Minnie back any more than you do. But we have to find a way to get Coveney to leave us alone. Otherwise, he'd be within his rights to charge us with kidnapping."

It seemed almost futile to argue. Charlie had a point. Technically, Margaret was under her father's care, and as such, he had the right to demand they return her. But as he pictured Angelique, he felt sick at the idea that it could be Minnie.

Hugh turned his gaze to Draven. "Maybe they are acting

on Coveney's orders. But we haven't heard from him to confirm it. How long can you keep them locked up?"

Draven appeared to be considering his words. "As long as it takes. But we have to find them first."

"They're not going to stop until they get her," Hugh said.

Chase patted Draven on the back. "I have no doubt he'll locate them. If the railroad men find out, they'll see that our town is a much safer place than some of the others they might be considering, where lawlessness happens all the time."

"We're going to need a bigger jail," Draven muttered.

With all the goings-on in Noelle lately, the jail had gotten more use in the past week than it had in months. Which was why they'd kept the sheriff so busy. Once Hugh had the chance to check on Minnie, he could help with the search.

A rustling sounded outside the door. Hugh stepped over to the window and peered out. Percival Penworthy was standing outside. He'd never liked the snake of a man. There was something about him that made his skin crawl. Penworthy hadn't noticed him, because he seemed intent on listening at the door.

Hugh motioned to the others, indicating they were being spied on. Charlie stepped to where he could see outside, but remain hidden. He swore under his breath.

"That's a good point about our town," Charlie said loudly. "We don't tolerate the same kind of troublemakers other towns do. You're right, Reverend. You as well, Hugh. Let's find these men and put them away."

At Charlie's words, Percival jumped back from the door. As Hugh opened it, he made himself look surprised at seeing him.

"Are you looking for the sheriff?" Hugh asked, grinning. "We're just finishing up."

Percival sniffed, and wiped at his nose the way he

constantly seemed to be doing. "No. I was looking for you. I noticed you were driving on that land of yours. I don't know why you don't want to sell, it's practically worthless, and I'm offering you a good price."

This again. One of the many reasons Hugh didn't trust Percival. If it was so worthless, why would Percival offer him a good price? Once the railroad came, his land was in a prime location. Something Percival obviously knew.

"I plan on building a house there come spring," Hugh said. "I'll need it for my wife and the family we hope to have."

Percival snickered. "I thought there was a problem with your bride. Isn't she a missing heiress? I believe there is a substantial reward for her safe return."

No one in town knew about the reward being offered for Margaret. So how did Percival? The others quickly picked up on Percival's words and the fact that they had deliberately hidden some of the information about Minnie.

"You're mistaken," Hugh said. "I know nothing of any reward."

Percival gave a nasty little grin that made Hugh want to punch him. "I heard it from the men her father sent to fetch her. They were discussing how they were going to spend the money."

One more reason not to hand Margaret over.

"It sounds like they were feeding you a line in hopes that you'd give them information about Margaret's whereabouts in exchange for money," Hugh said.

Draven stepped forward. "That's exactly what it sounds like. I have it on good authority that the father has a well-known policy of not paying out when it comes to his daughter. Too much of a temptation to kidnappers. You've been misinformed, and I hope you aren't spreading that misinformation."

Percival blew his nose. "If you say so. But if you think I'm going to stand in the way of Arthur Coveney being reunited with his beloved daughter, you should think again."

They already knew not to trust Percival, but now he'd made it clear where he stood. And yet, it wouldn't do to make him an enemy.

Hugh smiled at him pleasantly. "We feel the same way. We also hope for a joyous family reunion. Which is why we are doing everything in our power to see that Miss Coveney is safe and does not fall into the hands of anyone without her best interests at heart. Now if you'll excuse us, I believe we are all going to work toward that end."

The rest of the men all nodded, and went their separate ways, leaving Percival standing there, looking stunned. Hugh had said nothing to make it seem like they were opposing Coveney in any way. In fact, if his words were repeated to the man, it would sound as though Hugh and the others were in full support of Coveney.

He started toward his assay office, and Charlie jogged to catch up with him.

"Have you had a chance to look at the new ore I sent?"

He nodded. "I have. But let's go to my office to discuss where there aren't prying ears to hear."

As they walked, Charlie said, "I hope you know I have nothing against Minnie. It's obvious you're developing feelings for her. She seems like a nice woman, and if she weren't Arthur Coveney's daughter, I would fight for her alongside you. But you have to understand that opposing Coveney is suicide. Sometimes you have to carefully examine the merits of going into battle. Otherwise, you lose everything, even the very thing you're fighting for."

Hadn't Hugh given himself the same lecture?

"I know. It's why I'm doing my very best to keep her at arm's length. But even you have to admit that simply letting her go is not the right thing to do."

Charlie let out a long sigh. "I just hope our honor doesn't ruin us all."

Hugh unlocked the door to his office and let Charlie inside. "That's not the only thing you should be afraid of ruining us. The last ore you sent is of poor quality, with barely any gold. I know how hard things are for you, and I hate to be the bearer of bad news. But by the time you extract the gold, you will have barely paid for the labor to do so."

At least Charlie didn't appear surprised by his words. "Is there anything else of value? Based on the samples you're seeing, should we be trying in a different part of the mine? I can't give up. What else can we do?"

Hugh didn't want to tell Charlie that he'd already been testing the ore, searching for other minerals that might be valuable. So far, he hadn't found anything. But for Charlie's sake, for Noelle's sake, he would keep trying.

"I'll do what I can."

Charlie shook his hand. "Thank you. And thank you for keeping my business private. I don't want the men to lose hope."

"I understand the value of hope," Hugh said. "So, let's also do what we can to preserve hope for Minnie. Doesn't she deserve to have us do the right thing for her as well?"

He regretted the words as soon as they came out, because all they did was make Charlie look even more beaten-down.

"Maybe you're right. But I have too many other problems to solve to try to solve that one. If you find a solution that won't put Noelle in danger, I'll do everything I can to help you."

It was the best answer he could hope for, and only Hugh knew there still wouldn't be an easy solution. He'd already been trying, and failing, to come up with a viable idea.

As Charlie left, Hugh felt a deeper kinship with the other

man. Charlie would do anything to save Noelle, and Hugh was starting to think he would do anything for Minnie.

MINNIE FOLDED the blanket Birdie had lent her. Jack had used his woodworking skills to create a hidden nook for her to sleep in. The space was cramped, but safe. At least for now. She could hear voices in the other room.

"If she's not here, then you won't mind us taking a look around," a man's voice said.

Minnie placed the blanket inside the nook, then sealed herself back in. Though Jack had assured her no one would find her there, her heart thudded as footsteps came closer. Surely they could hear the sound of her beating heart.

"Like I said, she's not here," Jack stated. "I overheard her telling Birdie that she was going to go back with the mail wagon when it left today. Then she could get over the pass safely, and to the nearest town for the train. She said she just wanted to go home."

Minnie had to give Jack credit for his brilliance. By the time the men caught up to the mail wagon, they would already be in the next town, and it would be too late for them to come back to Noelle until tomorrow. But surely, when they did come back, they would be angry with Jack for his lie.

This had to stop.

Even though Birdie said she agreed with Minnie's decision, it wasn't right to put her friends and their businesses in danger.

Something crashed in the distance, like the men had knocked something over, looking for her.

"I told you she's not here. You have no right to come in here and ransack my business. Birdie, I believe the sheriff is looking for these men. If you and Gus could get him, my shotgun and I will keep them from doing any more damage."

Jack's voice gave Minnie some comfort, and even though Birdie had told her Jack would keep her safe, Minnie couldn't help wondering what helping her would cost her friends.

"Margaret," one of the men said in a singsong voice. "We know you're in here. Someone told us they saw you coming in yesterday, and no one's seen you coming out. Your daddy will be quite disappointed to hear the trouble you've given us. And I'm sure your fiancé will be displeased as well."

Another man murmured something that Minnie couldn't hear. The one who'd been speaking laughed.

"Lord Milliken does have some creative punishments for those who displease him. Has he shown you his whip yet? Or maybe his riding crop? Sometimes, when he gets bored with a girl, he lets me have a chance."

He was trying to scare her. Surely, he wasn't saying that Lord Milliken would whip her? Yes, he was trying to terrify her, because no gentleman would ever do such a thing.

Minnie closed her eyes.

"He's not going to let you have his intended. Not until he gets an heir." The other voice sounded almost upon her.

"So maybe we have her first. You're not stupid enough to talk, are you, Margaret?"

The sound of a shotgun being prepared to fire, or whatever it was they did, reached Minnie's ears. "No one will be having her," Jack said calmly. "I'd be happy to show you exactly what I mean, but I see the sheriff is almost here."

Something else clattered to the floor, and Minnie forced herself to remain calm. The real Minnie had told her Lord Milliken was capable of unspeakable things, and though Minnie had never understood the hints of whispers among servants, she fully understood now.

If only Minnie's heart wasn't beating so loudly. Nothing

on this earth could make her agree to marry Lord Milliken now. Surely if her father heard what these men were saying, he wouldn't make Margaret go through with it. But what if he did?

Her mother referred to the activities in the marital bed as humiliation. What these men spoke of was worse than that. And though none of the other ladies who traveled to Noelle with her told her anything about their wedding night, Minnie had to believe that none of them had endured the kinds of things these men were discussing. In fact, the women all seemed rather happy about the arrangement.

Earlier this morning, when Minnie had eaten breakfast with Jack and Birdie, the couple had exchanged glances and touches so full of love that Minnie had been so eaten alive with envy she had been unable to touch her food. She'd had a taste of that love yesterday with Hugh. He'd almost kissed her, she could tell, but his fear of her father's displeasure had stopped him.

What would it have been like to have had that moment with him? To feel his lips on hers the way she'd seen between Jack and Birdie?

Surely it would be too wonderful for words. And perhaps that was why none of the women ever spoke of it.

What seemed like hours later, Jack came to the alcove and let her out. "They're gone now. Sheriff Draven is taking them to the jail. He told me earlier that if they came back to send for him, and he would have them arrested for disturbing the peace. I don't know how long he can hold them, but for now, you're safe."

He gave her a smile, and though she knew it was meant to be reassuring, it only made Minnie feel worse. How much angrier would they be when they were released? They spoke of whips now, but what would happen when they were upset with her? What would they do to Birdie and Jack? Or even Hugh?

"Thank you," Minnie said. "I don't know what I would have done without you."

Jack's cheeks reddened. "It's the least anyone can do. We look out for our own, so it's no trouble. Hugh said he will come by for you in a little while."

Minnie's heart leap at the thought of spending more time with Hugh. Maybe today, she could convince him that she belonged here with him.

Birdie entered the room, and Jack put his arm around her. The look of affection that passed between them made Minnie even more certain about her feelings for Hugh. Hearing the fate that awaited her, and seeing that it didn't have to be that way, gave her hope that she and Hugh could have just as wonderful of a relationship.

"Did he give you any idea as to when that will be?" Minnie asked.

"I'm not sure," Jack said. "He has some things to do, and he wants to see if there is word from your father."

His words snuffed out the tiny flame of hope that had been flickering in Minnie's heart. Hugh was still determined to return her to her father. And now, more than ever, Minnie couldn't take the risk of her father being unsympathetic.

"That's all right," she said. "I don't mind waiting."

As she spoke, an idea hit her. "If the men are off to jail, it should be safe for me to go to his house, shouldn't it? Birdie helped me make some new curtains that will brighten the place up. I'd like to surprise him with them if I may."

Hopefully, they would agree it was safe for her to go. Alone. She wouldn't lie to her friends, they deserved better than that. So she would go, hang the curtains, scavenge a few supplies, and then do the very thing Jack had lied to the men about. She'd take the mail wagon over the pass, and get on the train. Only she wasn't going home. She would finally leave Margaret Coveney behind, and head somewhere where she could be Minnie Gold.

Birdie and Jack looked at each other like they weren't sure it was a good idea.

"You said Sheriff Draven took them to the jail. It will be safe enough to go to Hugh's house. I know he still isn't sure about marrying me. So maybe if I do something nice for him, it will help him make up his mind."

The sympathetic look Birdie gave her told Minnie she'd won. Birdie knew of Minnie's developing feelings for Hugh. Given her own recent success in love, she wouldn't deny Minnie a chance at happiness.

"All right. But let Jack walk you there. And stay there until Hugh returns."

Minnie nodded. "Of course. I just want to make Hugh happy."

The smile Birdie gave her made Minnie feel guilty. She'd write as soon as it was safe. But even that silent promise didn't make her feel better about misleading her friend. Still, as she gathered her things, Minnie did her best to act normally.

Once Jack left Minnie at Hugh's house, Minnie quickly hung the curtains, not wanting to waste any time. She could see the mail wagon at Birdie's preparing to leave Noelle, so she had to hurry. After rummaging through Hugh's desk, Minnie found some pen and paper, and wrote him a quick note, apologizing for the inconvenience, and asking him to beg Birdie's forgiveness on her behalf. It wasn't much, but it would have to do.

Minnie slipped out of the house and, careful that no one noticed her, climbed into the back of the mail wagon, situating herself underneath the bags of mail. Though she knew she must have taken several breaths in the time it took for the wagon to be on its way, Minnie didn't breathe easily until she'd felt the creak of the springs for several minutes.

It was a terrible thing, leaving behind such good friends. But how else was she to protect them? How else was she to avoid such a terrible fate? She'd heard whispers about the woman one of the men had hurt. Angelique. Hugh's friend.

The wagon stopped. Minnie lay very still, waiting to get underway again. She could hear the rustle of the flap in the back. Apparently, the wagon would have more stops before heading over the pass. Hopefully she wouldn't be discovered, but if she was, maybe the driver would be sympathetic to her situation.

"Minnie?" Hugh's voice startled her. "I know you're in there. I read your note. Please, come out."

How was she supposed to refuse him?

She moved to the bags of mail that had been covering her.

"I can't marry him," she said.

"I know."

The pained look on his face sent a glimmer of hope to herMinnie's heart.

"What are we going to do?" she asked.

"I don't know," he said, letting out a long sigh. "But your note scared me to death. I can't lose you. And yet, without your father's approval, I can't keep you."

She hated that he spoke the truth. Especially because he wore every bit of his torment on his face.

"Can we figure this out together?" he asked. "Will you trust me enough to find a way to help you that doesn't ruin us all?"

Given that she'd already been trying to do so, Minnie wasn't sure what other options they had. "What if there isn't one?"

Hugh shook his head. "There must be."

"And if there isn't?"

Maybe she was a fool to push the issue, but if there was any chance she would end up married to Lord Milliken, then she had to stay on this wagon.

Standing up straighter, he gave her a look that spoke of a deep promise. "Then we leave together. I don't want to leave Noelle and abandon my friends, but if it is our only option, then we'll go. There's a man in town who wants to buy my land, and though I hate to do it, I'll sell it to him, and along with what I have saved up, it will be enough for us to hide. But let us pray it doesn't come to that."

His voice shook as he spoke, and Minnie realized just how much he feared there wouldn't be a way for them to be together and remain in Noelle. Would it be worth it? Thinking about Birdie and Jack, Minnie would like to hope that she and Hugh would share the same happiness. But what if they were making a terrible mistake? Was she ruining Hugh's life just as much as she was ruining hers?

Hugh turned to her. "For now, we're going to let everyone think you succeeded in leaving. There's a place you can hide at my house if someone comes looking for you. You'll have to stay hidden, even more than you did at the freight office. Are you willing to do that?"

She was willing, but what if she was wrong? Still, Hugh had to have some faith that things would work out between them to take such a risk.

"Yes."

Hopefully she hadn't made the wrong decision.

CHAPTER 9

THE EIGHTH DAY OF CHRISTMAS

JANUARY 1, 1877

Hugh hated lying to his friends. But when he and Minnie had returned to town the day before, he'd taken Minnie to a secret storage room under his living quarters. He'd put it there for times when they had a great deal of gold and didn't want to draw anyone's attention to it. He kept the room a secret even from Charlie. And now, he was glad.

He had just gone to his work area to make sure no one was around before letting Minnie out again. Though he'd given her items for her comfort, she had to be going mad down there. As soon as he knew it would be safe, he'd go down and visit her, and bring her some breakfast. However, as he entered his office, he could see Draven at the door.

"Good morning," Hugh said, opening the door. "Any word of Minnie?"

The sheriff gave him an odd look. "Nope. I just figured I would come to check on things."

The other man stepped into the shop and looked around. Hugh didn't know what he was looking for, but there would be no sign of Minnie here. She'd left the note on his desk, which Hugh had already shown him, and he'd taken.

"Not much to check on."

Draven looked at the door to his living quarters. "I could use a cup of coffee."

"Of course."

Hugh led him into the room, looking around to make sure nothing was out of place, even though he'd been very careful to make sure there wasn't any sign of Minnie in the room.

He went to the stove and grabbed the pot that had already been simmering.

"I see I interrupted your breakfast," Draven said, pointing at the plate on the table.

He'd already eaten, because he'd been afraid that someone would stop by and see multiple dishes. At least he was right in cleaning up after himself before preparing something for Minnie.

"It's all right. To be honest, I'm not that hungry, worrying about Minnie. Would you like some? There's plenty to share."

"Just the coffee," Draven said. "But don't let me keep you from eating. Pearl made me a nice meal this morning, and I'd hate to see yours go to waste."

Hugh took a bite, and his stomach immediately complained in response. Then he set his fork down. "I just don't have much of an appetite."

Hopefully, he could get rid of him quickly so Minnie could eat. They'd had a filling supper, but she had to be hungry.

"We'll have more to worry about soon enough. I received

word from Arthur Coveney. He and Lord Milliken are coming to get Margaret personally. I'm not sure what we're going to do now that Margaret is missing."

Draven looked at him expectantly, like he knew that Hugh had something to do with Margaret's disappearance.

"Show them her note. I think it's clear enough that she left, and why."

The suspicious look didn't leave his face. "Jack and Birdie feel terrible. Birdie is nearly beside herself with worry over Margaret's safety. I'm surprised you didn't go after her."

"You didn't, either. We both know that by the time her note was found, it was too late to try to head over the pass. A man would get lost in the dark."

Draven stared at him. "So why didn't you go after her this morning?"

"How am I supposed to know which train she's getting on?"

"There aren't many trains, and you know it. What's really going on?"

The answer to his question wasn't as simple as it seemed. He couldn't tell the man the truth, not with Minnie's father on his way. But he also couldn't lie to his friend any more than he already had.

"You know more than I do. Just let me know how I can help with Coveney, and I'll do it."

Draven shook his head. "You can start by telling me where his daughter is."

"If I knew, I would tell you. But I don't." It wasn't exactly a lie. After all, Hugh didn't know exactly where Minnie was in the storage room. She could be on the little pallet she'd made up for herself as a bed, or she could be sitting on a chair.

"This is a dangerous game you're playing," Draven said. "I hope you know what you're doing."

He stood, and drained the rest of his coffee. "But just so

you know, if Coveney decides to file charges, I can't help you. At least, if you tell me the truth now, maybe we can figure a way out."

But there wasn't a way out. That was the problem. Especially not if both Coveney and her fiancé were coming.

"Thanks for the warning. Let me know when they arrive."

Hugh walked Draven out and watched as the other man headed down the street. The rest of the town seemed to be going about their usual business, which was a good sign. At least Hugh hoped.

He locked the door then went back to his living quarters where he locked that door as well. He was grateful for the curtains Minnie had hung, which gave him a little more privacy. He took the plate and use the secret trapdoor under his bed to get to her.

She had a small lamp and was using it to read. But when he came down, she closed her book and smiled at him. "I was starting to get worried."

"Sorry. Draven came to see me."

"I heard. What are we going to do about my father?"

Hugh still didn't know. But hopefully, something would present itself. He handed her the plate he'd prepared for her. "I'll talk to him when he gets here, see what I can do about changing his mind. Maybe he won't be as intent on having you marry Lord Milliken knowing the lengths you've gone to avoid it."

"I doubt it," Minnie said between bites. "I think he'll mostly be mad that I defied him. But I suppose it's worth a try."

He sat with Minnie for a while, enjoying her company as she ate. It would be nice to have her here with him always. Although it would be even better if she could have her out in the open. He hoped they could figure out a solution soon.

As Minnie finished her breakfast, Hugh heard footsteps

in front of his door. "I should go. It sounds like I have visitors."

He took her plate and climbed up out of the room, careful to make sure it didn't look like anything had been disturbed.

Before going to the door, he put the plate in the basin. When he peered out the window, he saw Charlie standing there.

He let Charlie in. "Do you have any new ore for me to look at?"

"Not at the moment. I'm here about Margaret. If you know where she is, you have to produce her. We don't want Coveney thinking we stand against him."

Surely someone would be an ally. Minnie was safe for now, but how much longer could Hugh keep her there without people figuring it out?

"As I told Draven, I'll do everything I can to help."

Charlie looked as doubtful as Draven had, but Hugh had made a promise to Minnie, and he had to help her. "Have you talked to the cook at *La Maison*? She was friendly with Minnie. Maybe she knows something."

"I don't have time to go chasing down people who might to know something about Margaret. I'm looking at the man who probably knows everything."

He supposed he did make it a little too obvious, at least where his feelings were concerned. Still, he wasn't going to give her up without a fight.

"Then I'll go talk to her. If Coveney and Lord Milliken are truly on their way, we'll need to see to their comforts anyway. I'll see what arrangements can be made for them at *La Maison* while I'm there."

If anything, it would at least keep everyone from continually stopping by. While he knew Minnie was hidden from view, the room had not been built with the intention of hiding a person in there. If she could hear everything being said, if she made a noise, someone might hear her.

"Let me walk with you. On our way, you can tell me how things are going at the mine." As they exited, he was careful to lock the door behind him. Hopefully it would deter anyone from entering and looking for Minnie on their own. He'd like to think that Charlie and Draven would never do such a thing, but then, Hugh had never thought he would have to lie to them either.

As they walked toward *La Maison*, Charlie filled him in on what had been happening at the mine. Nothing new or promising to report, but it was good to be kept up-to-date on things. Fortunately, it was a short walk, so he didn't have to continue feeling guilty for long.

When Hugh entered the building, Arabella accosted him almost immediately. "Where have you been? Why haven't you been seeing to my comforts?"

"Why are you still here? I thought I made it clear I wanted nothing more to do with you."

"And I told you that I won't be leaving without you. The family needs you."

"My place is here," he said, wondering if that would still be true after Coveney's visit. Even though Hugh had no desire to ever return to England, he had to consider it a viable option if he couldn't convince Minnie's father to call off her wedding.

Arabella gave one of her famous little pouts. "I need you."

There had to be more to her story than she was giving. And while he ordinarily wouldn't have had the patience for dealing with her drama, an idea hit. If she were to tell Coveney about what an important family they all were, even though Hugh's title was technically useless, it might be enough to impress the other man and consider Hugh's suit.

"Forgive me," he said, turning on his old charm. "I

haven't been as attentive to you and our family's needs as I should have been. Tell me what is going on, and how I can help. I have a little time before Margaret's father arrives to fetch her, and I hope you will assist me in entertaining him."

A wide smile filled her face. "She is going home then? And you are not marrying her?"

Oh, he would be marrying her, all right. But that was a part of his plan he couldn't yet admit to. "I believe that is what her father wants."

She gestured toward the parlor. "Then let's discuss how to impress Mr. Coveney, so the wedding will still happen. It wouldn't do for him to think that his daughter has been living in such horrible conditions. The groom might cry off if he knows how she has been compromised. But don't you worry, I will make sure they understand that everything has been proper, and that I have been a most excellent chaperone."

Playing on her need to get Margaret out of the way would make Arabella proud of how underhanded it was, if she wasn't the one being taken advantage of. But the more she rolled out the red carpet to impress Mr. Coveney, the more he might be willing to look upon Hugh as a prospective suitor. She was sure to go on and on about what an important family they were, and she was equally certain to put out her hopes for Hugh becoming the future duke. Only in this case, he wouldn't argue.

She went through the room, making small adjustments as she hummed to herself. Then she stopped. "But where is Margaret? She must be here so that I can demonstrate what an excellent chaperone I've been."

And that was the trouble. How could he bring Minnie out into the open at the risk of his plan failing? And what would his friends think if they knew he'd been hiding her all along?

"Leave that to me," he said. "I'm going to have a word with Milly."

Arabella made a noise. "That figures. Milly has been horrible to me this whole time. I overheard her telling Margaret she would help her hide, but you have to convince her that Margaret needs to return to our room so that it's all proper. We cannot afford the appearance of impropriety."

Hugh nodded, then took his leave. When he entered the kitchen, Milly was there, and not at all happy that he'd entered her domain.

"You're not welcome here."

"Minnie needs your help."

Milly looked startled, but then she wiped her hands on her apron. "In what way?"

"Her father and fiancé are coming. She's in hiding right now, and I'm supposed to produce her. I can't hand her over to them. But I need her here for my plan to work. I just don't know what I will do if my plan fails."

A thoughtful look crossed her face. "I told you I have a hiding spot. If things go bad, I can put her there."

Then she gave him a knowing look. "Where is she now? I heard she's gone missing. Charlie is furious because he thinks you had something to do with it. I didn't think you had the guts, so I'm happy to be wrong."

"I can't say. I'm still trying to work out how to produce her with the least amount of fuss."

Was that respect on her face? "I'll tell everyone she's been with me. Get her here, and I'll take care of the rest."

At least that was one problem solved. And hopefully a potential solution if Coveney was not impressed by Hugh's title.

"All right," he said. He started to leave, then stopped and looked at her. "What changed your mind about me? And why are you so eager to help her?"

"You called her Minnie. Plus, you wouldn't be hiding her if you didn't care for her. As for why I'm helping her, out of all the Society ladies I've ever known, Minnie has been the only one to treat me with respect. When I was a little girl, my mother worked in a house with a mistress like Minnie. She was kind to me, but her husband was a cruel man, and she often protected me from him. And when it was clear that he had his sights on me with bad intentions, she found me a safe place to go. Life hasn't always been good to me, but I've never forgotten that woman's goodness, and someone as good as Minnie deserves to be helped."

Hugh looked at the older woman and wondered if perhaps she wasn't as old as she appeared, but that life had just been that hard for her. "Are you happy here?"

"I'm happy enough, I suppose. It's not the worst place I've ever worked, and with all the goings-on here lately, it's been interesting. I'm a little sorry to see all the women get married, because then it will be back to dealing with Madame and her girls. I just hope the brides don't forget me now that they've started their new lives."

She looked tired and worn, and if Charlie did find a significant amount of gold, Hugh would take his earnings, and bring her to work for him. But that was a promise he couldn't rightly make, so he remained silent on that matter.

"We won't forget you. I'll make sure we come visit from time to time, and you're always welcome in our house."

Milly smiled at him. "You just keep that sweet girl from marrying a horrible man."

"I will."

MINNIE BREATHED in the fresh air, grateful to be back out in the open. Hugh had brought her to *La Maison*, where he explained that Milly was going to help her. She didn't like his plan, but she'd heard the pain in his voice as he'd lied to his friends. Yes, she wanted her freedom, and she appreciated his commitment to her. But even over the course of the day, she could see what it had cost him.

She closed her eyes as she leaned back against her chair outside the back door.

"Minnie!" Birdie's voice startled her. "I was so worried about you. What happened? Why did you run away?"

Minnie looked at her friend and took a deep breath. They had all agreed to say that Minnie had been here all along, but she hated lying to Birdie. Now she knew how Hugh had felt, and it made her feel even worse to know just how much everyone was sacrificing for her safety.

"I heard the men talking when I was hiding at your place. They spoke of doing horrible things to me, including using whips. I was terrified. The sheriff and the mayor wanted me to go back to my father because they were afraid that if they anger him, he'll use his influence to keep the railroad from Noelle. I couldn't bear the thought of hurting so many people, but I also cannot marry Lord Milliken."

Birdie came over and put her arms around Minnie. "Why didn't you say something? There are so many of us who would've helped you. Besides, those men are in jail. They can't hurt you."

Minnie gave her friend a squeeze, and it felt good to have her support. "They can't, but apparently Lord Milliken enjoys the same thing. I know my mother said the humiliation of the marriage bed is a woman's duty, but I cannot do it. Especially now that I've seen the happiness in so many of the other marriages in Noelle."

She looked down for a moment, hating to bring up such a personal topic. "I can't imagine that what you and Jack have is humiliating in any way. Forgive me for saying something so improper, but I just wanted you to know that you've given me hope I can find happiness."

Birdie laughed. "You poor thing. There's nothing improper about candid conversation between two close friends. No, there is nothing humiliating about my marriage bed. In fact, it's delightful, and I hope you will find the same."

Her friend's words made Minnie smile, and she turned her gaze back upward. "I think it will be that way with Hugh, delightful, that is. He is patient and gentle with me, and sometimes when I am with him, I feel things that seem…"

She shook her head, but Birdie smiled and squeezed her hand. "You care for him, don't you?"

"I do. But I don't know how we will ever be together. Hugh has a plan, but I'm afraid it won't work. What if it fails?"

Though Birdie smiled again, Minnie couldn't help the fear still swirling inside her.

"Don't lose hope," Birdie said. "Hugh has already sacrificed much for you. It's how I know he loves you too. I don't know how things will work out, but I know they will. I am living proof of that."

Hugh had said something similar to her earlier, and Minnie could only hope that they were both right. So far, none of her plans had worked out the way she had hoped.

The back door opened, and Hugh stepped out. "Arabella is looking for you. I know she's overbearing, and she will be even more so when your father arrives. But let her. These few moments are all she's going to have, because you have everything that matters most to me."

He turned his gaze to Birdie. "Thank you for coming by, and thank you for giving Minnie the encouragement she needs. You're a good friend, and your friendship will not be forgotten."

"It's my pleasure," she said. "And now I must be getting

back to Jack and Gus. But if there is anything you need, please don't hesitate to call on us."

They both nodded their assent, and when Birdie was out of view, Hugh held his hand out to Minnie. "Now let's go inside."

As she stood, he pulled her closer to him, almost into an embrace. "But first," he said softly, his breath tickling her cheek. "Let me reassure you that you have nothing to fear about our wedding night. I promise it won't be humiliating, and you will indeed find it delightful."

Minnie thought she might die of mortification that he had overheard their conversation. She tried to speak, but only vague sounds came out of her mouth.

Hugh pressed a finger to her lips. "You aren't allowed to be embarrassed. What will happen between us is perfectly wonderful and natural between a man and his wife when they are in love."

He hesitated as he pulled his hand away. Then he looked around. After a moment, he leaned into her again. "I do love you, Minnie. I hope my actions have shown that even if I haven't demonstrated as much in words. I have tried to keep my feelings at bay, but I cannot. However, as my plan unfolds, you may think me more indifferent than I am. Please know that, however things may look, my heart belongs to you, and only you."

For a moment, she thought he was going to kiss her like he almost had on their sleigh ride, but then he turned away. "This is not the right time," he said. "We must go inside before we are missed. From this moment on, you must return to the role of Margaret Coveney, as much as I know it will pain you. It is the only way to make my plan work."

Someday, Minnie would know what it was like to be kissed. To be held and loved by Hugh. She'd been embarrassed at her conversation with Birdie, but reassured by her friend's compassion. And Hugh's response to overhearing her words only made Minnie feel more confident. She wanted to know what her wedding night would be like with him. Hopefully they would find a way to make it happen soon.

CHAPTER 10

THE NINTH DAY OF CHRISTMAS

JANUARY 2, 1877

Minnie's father blustered in just in time to keep her from going absolutely mad at the way Arabella hovered. She had spent the past day listening to the woman talk nonstop about how Hugh was finally coming to his senses and accepting his rightful place at home.

"Margaret!" Her father embraced her warmly, and she stiffened. He'd never embraced her like that before. Had she been wrong in thinking his concern was merely about his business interest?

"It's good to see you, Father. I'm so sorry for the worry I have caused."

"But you're safe, and that's all that matters," he said. "And look who has come with me. Lord Milliken. He has been just as eager for news of you."

Margaret's slimy fiancé stepped forward, and Minnie

found him even more disgusting than ever. His thin frame and sallow skin were a stark contrast to the strength of Hugh standing next to him.

"How wonderful to see you again," she said, forcing a smile. Then she gestured to Arabella. "May I present to you both my companion, the Duchess of Hallstead?"

She stood, and practically preened like a peacock. "Please. You must all call me Arabella. We're in America now, and among friends. Isn't that right, Lord Hugh?"

Minnie could tell that Hugh was fighting irritation at being referred to by his title. But he smiled. "Indeed. Which is why I must insist that you all simply call me Hugh."

Lord Milliken made a face. "I cannot get used to this American custom of referring to people by their names. Your Grace, it is a delight to make your acquaintance. I often saw you and your husband in passing in London, and I always thought you were one of the loveliest of all English roses. I had envied your husband for having such a beautiful wife."

"I am a widow," Arabella said, fanning herself in such a simpering way that Minnie could hardly believe her father and Lord Milliken were eating it up. "My dear husband passed away recently, and I'm here to fetch Hugh home, as he is in line to be the next Duke of Hallstead."

The brazen words made Hugh's jaw twitch, and Minnie longed to give him comfort. Once again, Arabella was pushing aside three people he cared about and assuming he would take their place. He'd explained to Minnie that the only way that would happen was if all three of them died. What an awful thing to wish upon one's sons and brother-in-law.

However, Margaret's father looked intrigued. "A duke, you say? What is it that you are, Milliken? I always forget the English titles and such. I'm sure my wife could explain it to me, but she isn't here. Are we supposed to bow?"

Hugh shook his head. "Please don't. I believe Lord Milliken is an earl, which is of lower rank than a duke, but as I have said, let us not stand on ceremony. Instead, we shall all be equals, conversing as friends."

It was quite enjoyable, watching Lord Milliken be put in his place, especially since her father gave him a funny look.

"That sounds mighty fine to me," Margaret's father said. "I have been dreading taking my daughter to England, because I can never get the addresses and treatments of peers correct. But my wife has always said only a lord would do for our daughter, and that is just what we found."

He looked over at Milliken, and the man puffed his chest, making himself look rather silly. It wouldn't just be the wedding night that would be humiliating with a man like Lord Milliken. It would be spending every single day of her life with him.

"She should have set her sights higher," Arabella said. "But I can understand not knowing the various ranks. For me, I always knew that only a Duke would do. And look at me now."

Once again, she preened, full of so much self-importance, it was hard for Minnie to understand how Hugh could have ever been in love with her.

"I didn't know about the duke," Margaret's father said. Then he turned and looked at her. "Would you prefer a duke, my dear?"

Was he making a joke? Right in front of Lord Milliken, with whom he'd already signed contracts?

Minnie opened her mouth to answer, but then Hugh caught her eye and shook his head. Apparently, she wasn't allowed to be honest. "I think this is not the time to discuss my marriage plans, especially since agreements have already been made."

"Yes," Lord Milliken said. "Agreements have been made, which is why I don't understand why you ran away like this."

Margaret's father looked at her expectantly. She should have known she wouldn't get off so easily.

"I'm sorry. I was afraid. I'd heard Lord Milliken had mistreated one of our maids, and it made me fearful."

Milliken made a noise, like he thought she was being ridiculous. And even Margaret's father looked at her like she was making a big deal out of nothing.

"And then, the horrible men who came here looking for me, they said Lord Milliken would use his whip upon me. I was terrified. I must have every assurance that such a thing will not happen."

At least that got her father's attention. "What's this about a whip?" He looked at Milliken, who shrugged.

"I've never heard such a thing in my life. I'm sure those men were lying. Probably outlaws trying to get the reward for themselves, and willing to say anything to make Miss Margaret come with them."

She knew they hadn't been lying. Nor had Minnie lied. And the look in Milliken's eyes told her that he was the one not telling the truth.

"You can ask them," Minnie said. "They're in the jail for beating one of the ladies."

Hugh made a noise, and when Minnie looked at him, he gave her a sharp look.

"Dear, we do not talk about those women," Arabella said. She looked at Margaret's father. "You know the sort of woman I'm speaking of. Poor Margaret has been in this rough place for so long that I fear she has forgotten some of the conventions of Society."

Though Margaret's father nodded, he wore a strange expression upon his face. Did he realize that there was more to the story, and to Lord Milliken, then he knew?

"I have made good friends here," Margaret said. "Maybe the people aren't of the sort of consequence we might think, but they are the sort of people I'm proud to know. They are honest, hard-working, and kind."

She turned to her father and smiled. "You will not find better people than I have found in Noelle. Though I know I was wrong in running away, I am glad to have come here and made so many good friends."

Her father looked pleased at her words, and it gave Minnie hope that perhaps Hugh's plan might work after all.

"A duchess and the heir to a dukedom are fine friends to have," Lord Milliken said. "They will be welcome in our home always. But I do not think the rest of the people in this town are the sort one should associate with. It would be frowned upon in our society."

Arabella nodded. "You are quite right. Scandalous pasts, and if word got out about Margaret's association with such people, I don't think people would look at her the same. Fortunately, I have been here to guide and chaperone her so that nothing untoward will stain her good reputation."

No wonder Hugh didn't want to return to England.

Then Arabella patted the chair next to her. "Come, sit with me, Lord Milliken. I wish to hear of your acquaintances in London. Once you and Margaret are married, I cannot wait to introduce her to Society. No doors are closed to the Duchess of Hallstead. Once Hugh inherits, you will both find a great deal of friendship, worthy friendship, with important people who can clear the way for many things."

As Lord Milliken sat, he practically drooled with avarice. He and Arabella were two of a kind, and they belonged together. Hugh hadn't been entirely clear on his plan when he spoke of it to Minnie, but she had to wonder if this was part of it. Did he suspect that Lord Milliken and Arabella would be attracted to one another, and it would somehow make Lord Milliken cry off? Arabella would be stupid to give up her plans for Hugh in favor of a penniless Earl, but Lord Milliken might be easier to get to do her bidding.

"Smart as well as beautiful," Lord Milliken said. "I am sure you will be a wonderful guide for Margaret. She has much to learn about the ways of the world, and I most grateful that someone like you would take her under your wing."

Minnie looked at her father. Was this what he wanted for her? His brow was furrowed, like he was trying to puzzle something out. Hopefully he could see the ridiculousness of this arrangement.

"That does sound lovely," Minnie said. "I had feared not having friends when I moved to England. It will be nice to have Arabella, and I hope, Hugh. Hugh has proved himself to be a true and faithful friend, and it is my deepest wish that we can continue our friendship in England."

Her father smiled at her indulgently. Then he glanced at Hugh. "Thank you for taking such good care of my daughter."

Lord Milliken however, did not share the same happiness with the situation. "Just what sort of friend were you? You did not take any liberties, did you? It would be a terrible thing if you compromised my bride."

Hugh smiled. "I took no liberties. It would be dishonorable to do so, and a young lady such as Margaret deserves to be treated well. I could not bear it if anyone thought I had mistreated her."

"I am glad to hear it," her father said. "You hear such tales of roughness in towns like this. Such an uncivilized place."

With another broad smile, Hugh said, "It is easy to think that, having never been here. We are in talks with the railroad to have a spur brought into Noelle. And I'm sure, if you spent time here, especially once the railroad comes, you would be quite impressed at how this town has grown. I'm very proud to be part of the development of Noelle, and how we are shaping it into the kind of place many people can call home."

He sounded like an advertisement, but then Minnie remembered that Hugh was hoping her father would speak kindly about Noelle to the railroad people and not harbor a grudge over Margaret's time here.

Her father nodded. "I like the sound of that. People coming together to create a town of respectability and enterprise. I've been part of many such projects. In fact, I came to Denver when it was just a speck on the map, and now look at it. I can see why you would want to be here, not in stuffy old England. It's too bad you're going home to be duke. It's my only regret in allowing Margaret to marry Lord Milliken. Having her so far away."

It seemed odd to have her father speak of her with such affection. He'd never done so before. But perhaps, the thought of losing her had brought a change to his heart. Maybe she had been too pessimistic in thinking that he wouldn't let her call off her wedding. Was there hope that she could marry Hugh after all?

HUGH TRIED NOT to jump for joy as he watched Arabella and Lord Milliken flirt. He couldn't believe both of them were being so obvious, especially in front of Margaret's father. And Coveney was clearly aware of the impropriety. As Arabella played with the locket around her neck, Lord Milliken practically licked his lips as he focused her gaze on her ample bosom. For a moment, Hugh thought that Coveney would jump up and pull the man away.

Arabella had already perfectly set the stage by explaining that Hugh's eventual title was better than Milliken's. And now, he was having doubts about the kind of man his daughter would be marrying.

But was it enough to get him to call off the wedding and let Hugh marry her instead? The trouble was, he would have to eventually tell Coveney that the chances of Hugh ever becoming Duke were slim, especially now that Hugh had heard from his brother Gerald. He'd gotten the wire yesterday. Gerald had told him Arabella was suspected of killing John, but they had no proof. She'd been asked to leave the estate and given a home and an allowance in London contingent upon her leaving her sons alone. It was enough information for him to realize that Arabella hoped that if she could convince him to come back, she would be welcomed as well. And then she could make her sick dream of getting Hugh to be Duke a reality. If she'd killed John, she wouldn't hesitate in killing others.

Minnie and her father had begun conversing about her time in Noelle, leaving Arabella and Milliken to continue in their flirtation. The longer Hugh was in the room with Margaret's intended, the more certain he was that she should never be forced to marry him. Arabella, on the other hand, deserved such a fate.

"Hugh, could we take my father on a tour of the town? I especially want him to see the assay office. You do such fine work there, and I found it fascinating to hear about how you value the gold and determine the mineral content of various rocks. Who knew that there is so much more to a rock than it being a rock?"

He gave them a smile. "You know I can't refuse you anything." But he turned to her father. "I don't wish to bore you, but if you would find it interesting as well, I am happy to show you around. We can also meet our mayor, Charles Hardt, the Reverend Chase Hammond, and Sheriff Draven, who all played a role in keeping your daughter safe."

Coveney glanced over at Milliken and Arabella, who both seemed so engrossed in each other that they'd forgotten where they were. Then again, they were in a brothel, so perhaps they were acting entirely appropriately, given the location.

"I think that's a fine idea. Though it may be cold, I think the fresh air will do us all some good. Lord Milliken, will you join us?"

He looked over at Coveney. "You know I cannot stand the cold. I do not wish to catch a chill. You go on and enjoy yourselves. Perhaps Arabella could have the servants bring us some tea."

For a man who'd been so insistent upon propriety, he'd certainly begun using Arabella's first name rather quickly. The expression on Coveney's face told Hugh that the older man had noticed as well. It seemed his plan was working. But he wasn't going to count himself the victor until his ring was on Minnie's finger.

Arabella stood. "That sounds like a fine idea. I, too, despise the cold. And the streets are filthy. Certainly no place for a lady. However, I do understand why Margaret would want her father to see where she's been staying."

He could not have planned this more perfectly. Arabella and Milliken would be left alone, and given the chemistry already happening between them, things were bound to happen. But would it be enough for Milliken to think Arabella a better prize than Margaret? A duchess, even a widowed one, would give him clout. But he doubted Arabella's allowance would be enough to keep Milliken happy for long. Margaret's purse was deeper. Which one did Milliken value more? And would it matter if Margaret's father continued to look so displeased at Milliken's behavior?

They exited the brothel, and Hugh led them through town, pointing out various landmarks and businesses that might be of interest to Arthur Coveney. The air had gotten chilly, even more so than usual, and Hugh knew they couldn't stay out long. But it was such a delight watching Minnie chatter about all the things she loved about Noelle, and her father nodding appreciatively.

Hugh pointed at the mine, and then they walked to his office. He gave them a brief tour, and as he was explaining how his furnace worked, Coveney stopped him.

"You have no intention of going back to England, do you?"

He knew this conversation would have to happen at some point, but he'd hoped it wouldn't be so soon. Not before he was confident that Coveney would accept his suit.

But there was something about the man that made Hugh unwilling to be dishonest.

"Unfortunately, I don't. Arabella was hoping to convince me, but honestly, all she does is remind me of all the reasons why I like it better here."

The other man nodded slowly. "You would give up being a duke to remain here?"

How did he explain that there was little to no chance he would ever become duke? And that he didn't want to.

"There are others perfectly capable of doing the job far more competently than I can. I am happy here, and my family is happy with how things are in England. Arabella is the only one who wishes for things to be different."

"I gather she was your brother's wife?"

Hugh nodded. "I'm sure it makes her think she has some obligation to run the family. But it is not necessary."

"And it would be imprudent for you to marry her," Coveney said. "A man should not marry his brother's widow."

Was it possible that Coveney was starting to consider Hugh a proper husband for his daughter?

"That, and Arabella and I would never suit. I wish for a wife who values kindness, hard work, and honor above a person's rank or status. Most importantly, I want someone who will be a true companion to me so we can build a life together."

All of the reasons he cared for Minnie. Yet none of the reasons Coveney had for marrying off his daughter. How could he convince him that he would be a far better husband than Lord Milliken?

"But you're still Lord Hugh, right?"

Hugh nodded. If the title was what really mattered to him, Hugh would use it for Minnie's sake. "But I think, in America, those titles matter less than a man's character. I would be proud for my wife to carry my title, but I would be most proud of her character."

"You're a good man, Lord Hugh. I hope you someday find a wife who fits your needs, and you don't have to do another silly mail-order arrangement. It must be very disappointing to send for a wife who cannot be your wife, but I think in the end, you will be better for it."

So that was it then. Coveney wasn't going to let him marry his daughter, at least not now. But he would find a way- he had to find a way- to make the man understand that Margaret was everything he needed, and he would be everything for her.

They returned to the brothel, and he could sense that even Minnie felt slightly dejected over the conversation they'd had. He'd hoped for Coveney to see that his daughter deserved an honorable man, and that Hugh was that man. Had he been wrong to admit that he had no plans to return to England and become duke?

When they got to the front porch, Milly was waiting. She put her finger to her lips, then opened the door and beckoned them in. They'd barely stepped into the foyer when they could clearly see in the parlor that Lord Milliken and Arabella were engaged in a very inappropriate activity.

Minnie gasped, and Hugh quickly grabbed her by the shoulders and turned her away.

"I realize that is a shocking sight, so please, look no more."

Coveney stormed into the room. "I know a man has needs, but are you such a disgrace that you would so publicly dishonor my daughter?"

The pair straightened, tugging at their clothing back into presentable shape, but even if they'd put things in place, the damage had been done.

"I'm sorry," Milliken said. "I don't know what came over me."

Minnie moved out of Hugh's grasp and stepped into the room. "Father, you cannot possibly expect me to him marry a man like this. I have been betrayed in the worst way, and it would be cruel to continue with this farce."

A few tears fell from her eyes, and though Hugh disliked women who used tears to manipulate, he was grateful that Minnie was doing so now. Coveney looked absolutely distraught at the sight.

"My dear," Milliken said, still adjusting his pants. "It was a momentary aberration, and I can assure you it won't happen again."

Minnie glared at him. "I saw you leaving a house of ill repute in Denver. When I told my mother, she said it was something all men did. But I cannot turn a blind eye to this."

Then she turned back to her father. "You should speak with the men in the jail, who intimated that this type of behavior is common to Lord Milliken. Is this what you want for me? Because I cannot live in such a way."

Coveney nodded slowly. "It seems I may need to ask a few more questions." He glanced over at Milliken. "We may have a contract, but I will speak with my lawyers, because it can easily be broken based on your actions. You have done a most cruel thing to my daughter. You had to have known we would be returning soon. Do you have so little self-control that you would take such a risk?"

It was one of the things Hugh had most hoped for. He knew Arabella thrived on the thrill of getting caught. And with as reckless as Milliken seemed to be, Hugh had hoped that if there was a spark between the two, he would be willing to do the same. At least this part of the plan was working beautifully.

Now he just had to find a way to convince Coveney that despite Coveney's doubts about Hugh, he was the perfect husband for Margaret. And Margaret could finally fully become Minnie.

CHAPTER 11

THE TENTH DAY OF CHRISTMAS

JANUARY 3, 1877

Minnie couldn't believe the shameful state of affairs. Though she had been whisked away immediately upon discovering Arabella and Lord Milliken, she knew what had transpired. How could she not? Everyone knew, and her father had spent the rest of the evening locked in a room with Lord Milliken.

Hugh had told her to be patient, and that all would be well, but she had never seen her father so angry.

Arabella must have been sent to another room, because she never returned to the one she and Minnie had shared. Which left her waking alone and unsure of facing the day ahead of her. Hugh had told her to trust in him and his plan. But so far, everything seemed to be falling apart.

Her father had said nothing about her impending marriage.

Could she bear it if he still wanted her to marry Lord Milliken? What had been the result of them spending so much time shut in a room together?

As much as she wanted to delay facing everyone, she knew she had to do it at some point. She dressed slowly, carefully. Was it too late to run away?

A knock sounded at her door. "Margaret, are you dressed?"

Her father. Too late to run away after all. "Come in."

As he entered, she could see the lines on his face and dark shadows under his eyes. It comforted her to know her father had also endured a sleepless night. But the question was, why?

"Lord Milliken isn't the man I thought he was," he said, looking far older than his years. "I met with Sheriff Draven and talked to the men Lord Milliken had sent for you. Lord Hugh had also made inquiries into Lord Milliken, and I am greatly troubled by the reports I've been given."

Minnie nodded slowly. "I think, if you were to ask our servants, assuring them that there would be no reprisals, they would also tell you he is not a good man."

Her words only seemed to make her father look more upset. "How did I miss it?"

"You and Mother would only consider a lord for my future husband. In all the times we spoke of my future, not once did you specify you wanted me to marry a good man."

Her father's face turned ashen. "I would've thought that would be understood."

"You shouldn't assume," Minnie said. "Until you came looking for me, I believed you saw me only as one of your possessions. You sought to increase your empire, not pursue your daughter's happiness."

As she spoke, she could feel the strength of Minnie emboldening her. Margaret would never have spoken to him like that. She would have been too fearful of his wrath and of displeasing him. Everyone was afraid of her father, including the men of Noelle. Perhaps they were not brave enough to stand up to him, but somehow, in all of this, Minnie had found the strength.

"I don't suppose I saw it that way," he said quietly. "You have to believe that everything your mother and I have done has solely been for you."

"Perhaps you should have asked me what I wanted."

She squared her shoulders as she looked at him, unafraid of the consequences. "You and Mother isolated me so much that, until coming here, I knew nothing of the world."

"We only wanted to protect you," he said.

"From having friends? My only friend in the world was my maid. I wasn't allowed other acquaintances, because you and Mother were afraid I'd become associated with the wrong people. In protecting me, you kept me from many of the joys of life."

For once, her father looked like he was actually listening to her. She took a deep breath as she continued. "Coming to Noelle has been the greatest gift, because I finally know what it is like to have friends. A woman who would give me precious material she needed for her livelihood, so I wouldn't freeze to death. And then, when those horrible men were looking for me, she hid me, so they wouldn't find me, even though they threatened her husband and their business. I became friends with a cook who taught me what she knew, so I would be able to survive on my own. She also put herself at risk to protect me."

Her eyes filled with tears as she realized the kind of friends she'd made. But there was one friend, one even more dear to her that her father must hear about.

"But most importantly, there was Hugh. He accepted me despite all my flaws. Was willing to marry me, even though I was not the woman he'd thought me to be. And then, when he learned the truth about my identity, his honor was such that he chose to protect me and care for me."

The memory of their almost kisses came back to her, and she finally understood why Hugh had held back. "He put my needs before his own, and when he realized what a horrible man I was marrying, he was willing to risk everything to keep me safe, even from Lord Milliken."

That was love. Hugh would have given up everything for her, and had demonstrated time and again that he would always do the right thing when it came to how he treated Minnie.

"You care for him." His words were a statement of fact, and yet they did not go far enough.

"I love him." She looked at her father, hoping she could somehow convey the depth of her feelings for Hugh. But more was at stake here.

"In order for the railroad to come to town, twelve marriages were supposed to take place. Nine have happened so far. Hugh and I were to be one of the twelve, but he is too honorable to marry me without your consent. He made that decision as soon as he found out I was a young lady of means, and not a maid. How many men would have taken advantage?"

Her father looked thoughtful. "The Mayor did make mention that they were eager to gain the railroad's business. But what does any of the have to do with me?"

Surely, he could not be so blind as to not see it? But then he nodded slowly. "My coal. But I have no say in where the railroad decides to build a spur or not."

She shook her head. "You have a reputation for your vindictiveness. Everyone thought if you believed the town was involved in my plan to leave Lord Milliken, and I married Hugh without your consent, you would be angry and, out of revenge, convince the railroad not to come here."

For a moment, he looked surprised, and then he nodded slowly. "I can see where they would have thought that. And had I not come here myself, to see where you had gotten off to, I could also see where I might have done such a thing."

"But you won't, will you?" Had she appealed to his sense of reason enough that he could understand that all the choices in the situation that he would view as being wrong were hers and hers alone? "Once they learned my true identity, they did everything they could to keep me safe until I could be returned to you. I was the one who fought to stay."

She left out the part about Hugh, since she didn't want to give away just how much he'd been willing to do for her. Especially since she wasn't sure if they would end up having to run away.

"Do you still want to stay?" He looked at her, and his eyes seemed to reflect an expression of genuine desire to understand her wishes.

"With all my heart. I love it here, and I want…" Minnie closed her eyes and took a deep breath. Had she asked too much?

"I want for you to consent to my marriage to Hugh. Before the railroad's deadline."

He pursed his lips and looked thoughtful for a moment. "Is your marriage still about saving Noelle, or is it something more?"

"You were going to marry me off to a man who needed my fortune to save his estate. Why would my answer matter now?"

An unfamiliar expression drifted across his face. "Because it does. I very nearly made a mistake in not asking that question before, and I will not risk giving you to a monster again."

At least she knew without a doubt that he no longer intended for her to marry Lord Milliken. Which should have been a victory, except now she wanted more.

"I cannot answer for Hugh, but while it is my dearest wish for Noelle to survive, I also could not imagine a life without him by my side."

"I see," he said, but he did not elaborate, and as they sat in a longer silence than felt comfortable, Minnie could only hope it was because he was considering what she'd said.

HUGH STOOD outside Minnie's door, unable to believe the conversation he was hearing. She loved him. Enough to stand up to her father and tell him what she really wanted. Him.

He opened the door and entered the room.

"And I wish to marry Minnie. I mean, Margaret." He looked at her, then back at Coveney. "Not just to save Noelle, even though that was one of my initial motivations. Nor is it for companionship, which was my other reason for choosing a mail-order bride. But because there is no other woman I wish to companion me for the rest of my life than your daughter. She is kind, willing to learn, loyal, and someone with whom I greatly enjoy spending my time."

Coveney nodded with every good quality Hugh listed. But he knew those were not the things Coveney most desired in a husband for his daughter.

"I realize I am not a lord in my own right, not as you had hoped. I had always said I have no desire to return to England and to live my life as part of Society. But if it would mean you looking more favorably upon my suit, then perhaps we could find a compromise, where we would spend part of the year in England, and the rest of the time, we could be here. I would live anywhere if it meant doing so with Minnie."

Minnie came to stand beside him, looking at him with such love that it didn't matter what Coveney said. They'd already agreed to defy him, but for the sake of the older man before them, he hoped they could come to an agreement. Regardless of what happened in this room, Hugh would marry her. The question was, would it be done in such a way as to help Noelle?

"You call her Minnie, as does everyone else," Coveney said slowly. "Why, when you know she is really Margaret?"

Hugh looked over at the woman he loved, and considered how much she had grown in her time in Noelle. "Because she has become a new person. A woman who chooses her own fate, and wishes to be acknowledged as such."

Coveney nodded slowly. "You have my blessing to marry Margaret. I thought an advantageous match would ensure her happiness, but it seems I knew nothing of what would make my daughter happy at all. Though my wife wanted Margaret to be a lady, she was despondent at the prospect of having her living so far away. If you both remain in Noelle, she will be able to visit with ease. Especially if the railroad goes through. The trek over the mountain is treacherous in a wagon, and my wife is not strong enough to make it."

He smiled at them. "I cannot make any promises as to the outcome, but I will have a word with some people I know and see if I can't do some persuading. Anything for my family."

"Thank you," Hugh said. "I hope you know that's not what we're asking, but we do appreciate anything you do on Noelle's behalf."

"My wife despaired of never seeing her grandchildren. If I can make it easier for that to happen, we will all be happier for it. Are you sure we can't wait for her to come to the wedding?"

Minnie put her arm around Hugh. "We've waited long enough already. But you will be there, and you can tell Mother that she may plan a reception for us in the spring in Denver."

Hugh smiled down at her, then turned his gaze back upon Coveney. "Be sure to have the papers write it up as a love match with a lord."

He never imagined he'd use his title again, but to make his soon-to-be wife's family happy, it was a small price to pay. Especially since the older man's eyes were shining.

"When will the wedding happen?" Coveney asked.

"Right now," Margaret said. "We've put it off too many times, and I will not have anything stop it again."

Within a couple of hours, they were all congregated at the saloon in front of the lopsided Christmas tree Hugh and some of the men had found to welcome the ladies to Noelle. Though they hadn't had many ornaments, Hugh noticed their number had grown. There was an interesting one that looked a lot like a lord. But that was just fancy on his part, he was sure.

So much had happened today that he almost wasn't sure he'd be able to remember his own name upon reciting his vows. Charlie had brought him some new ore to test before the wedding, and while the tests were not yet complete, Hugh had a glimmer of hope that there might be something worthwhile to be found. After all, hadn't he found a way to marry Minnie against all odds?

And then he'd had to visit Arabella. She had wept when he'd told her, but he was sure they were mostly crocodile tears, since Lord Milliken was on hand to comfort her. The two had then ridden out of town, presumably to start new lives together. Hopefully, she would realize that her dreams of controlling the family were now over, and she'd finally get what was coming to her.

What mattered most was that he and his love were there, standing in front of the Reverend, promising to love one another until death parted them. Though Minnie was frustrated at not having married him in the very beginning, Hugh was grateful they'd had this time to realize that their marriage was far more than mere convenience. The plan to save Noelle and maybe stave off some of his loneliness had turned into so much more.

Especially since Arthur Coveney stood beside them, beaming proudly.

Hugh couldn't have imagined things working out more perfectly. And fortunately, since they were celebrating a wedding morning, their wedding night could last all day.

EPILOGUE

THE ELEVENTH DAY OF CHRISTMAS

JANUARY 4, 1877

When Minnie woke, she cuddled up to Hugh, who gave her a lazy smile.

"How are you feeling today?"

She smiled back. "Wonderful."

"Not humiliated?"

His chest rumbled with his laugh, and it made her feel safe and warm.

"No," she said. "I don't know why any woman would think it was. I can't imagine what my mother must have been thinking, telling me that."

He kissed the top of her head. "I could have a talk with your father. Maybe he could use a few suggestions."

Minnie sat up and stared at him. "You wouldn't!"

They'd already had an uncomfortable conversation with

her father. She couldn't imagine one of such a personal nature.

Hugh gave her a lingering kiss that tingled in places she couldn't imagine still tingling after last night. Whatever adventure life took them on, spending it with Hugh was going to be worth all the struggles that had brought them there.

WHAT'S NEXT

January 4, 1877
  Noelle, Colorado
  In the midst of this most chaotic day, I find my thoughts drifting to all that has transpired this week. Each of the couples thus far wedded to satisfy the agreement between the town and the railroad have most miraculously resulted in a happy conclusion-the good Reverend and Felicity, Culver, Kezia and sweet little Jemimah have formed a family that warms my heart. Meizhen and Woody— such devotion I've not seen in couples married for years. I see how Birdie has changed Jack's demeanor, how Gus's step seems lighter since I first arrived. Sheriff Draven and Pearl-a most unlikely match to eyes who cannot see the passion and loyalty between them. Even Maggie and Storm have been able to overcome the obstacles they faced a few days ago to create a union including Ezra, and not one—but two—lovely geese. What is there that love cannot do when challenged? If one needs proof, look only at Liam and Avis, or Cara and Doctor Deane. I've seen how Nacho looks at Fina with adoration and pride, and how Minnie and Hugh found each other through such adversity. Though my heart is joyous for

each, I am hopeful for each of my brides to find the happiness they so richly deserve.

Yet, I confess, I cannot help but hear the faint beating of my own hearts desires. I have for years thought myself immune, able to hide away my feelings in lieu of helping make others happy. But of late, I have found myself thinking of the young soldier whom I fell in love with at first sight. True, it's silly to entertain such thoughts.

Yet his touch lingers still in my mind, his kiss in my soul. I wonder what became of him or if he's ever given another thought about me. These are but musings, I realize, but it presses the question—am I destined to walk this life alone?

Genevieve Walters

A determined matchmaker, a stubborn mountain man...and only two days left to save the town! *Find out Genevieve's fate in* THE PIPER; Day Eleven!!

If you've missed any of the Twelve Days of Christmas Mail-Order Brides, you can find a complete listing here: http://amzn.to/2kAn6S0

READER LETTER

Dear Reader,

I was super excited to be invited to be part of this project. I was the last author to join, so I was given the Tenth Day: The Lord. And wow, talk about everything working out perfectly. With such a title, I knew I had to incorporate a lord, and I've always loved stories about people with titles coming to America and living a new life. On top of that, because Noelle is based on Leadville, Colorado, I already knew much of the area and history, thanks to my love of that area. I have several books set during Leadville's mining boom, so this was a natural fit. I've always wanted to write about an assayer, so getting to put in that tidbit was a real treat. There were so many other little things I got to put in the story that were all things I've always wanted to do. Which made this one of the most fun projects I've worked on.

But that wasn't the best part. I'm hoping that you've read the other stories in this series and love them as much as I do. Working with the other authors was an absolute joy, and I cannot say enough good things about a terrific group of writers. I'm so grateful they invited me to be part of this project, and I hope we can all work on something else together in the future.

All of this came at a very dark period in my life. I can honestly say this has been one of the worst years I've had. However, this project, and this amazing group of authors, was one of the bright spots that kept me going.

I hope, whatever you're going through, if you're having a rough time, you can find little things, like I did with this project, to remind you of the good in this world.

Danica Favorite

To the rest of the MOB authors, it's truly been an honor working with you, and I love you all.

Special thank you to Sara Benedict for all of her help in keeping us organized!

ABOUT THE AUTHOR

A self-professed crazy chicken lady, Danica Favorite loves the adventure of living a creative life. She and her family recently moved in to their dream home in the mountains above Denver, Colorado. Danica loves to explore the depths of human nature and follow people on the journey to happily ever after. Though the journey is often bumpy, those bumps are what refine imperfect characters as they live the life God created them for. Oops, that just spoiled the ending of all of Danica's stories. Then again, getting there is all the fun.

Subscribe to Danica's newsletter for all her latest news

You can connect with Danica at the following places:

Amazon BookBub Instagram

www.danicafavorite.com/